ADVANCE PR

"**Refreshingly original writing with a delightful** twist. ...author [Jim] Story proves to be **a master of the slow reveal,** gradually pulling away the veil that shrouds a secret that's central to the plot. ...a smartly conceived, **beguiling tale that few readers will forget.**"

—*Kirkus Reviews*

"[A] **haunting** story of a man possessed by a fascination with birds and a fear of the past which he's worked so hard to bury.... **Steeped in natural beauty and interpersonal connections....**"

—D. Donovan, Senior Reviewer, *Midwest Book Review*

"In *The Condor's Shadow* Jim Story **masterfully takes us into the mind of a man** you've probably seen on the street, maybe worked with, shared a passing smile. A man on the run from the skeletons in his past. **Get to know him. I did and I'll never forget him.**"

—Celeste Rita Baker, author of *Back, Belly & Side: True Lies and False Tales*

"**When I saw I only had twenty-three pages left to read** of Jim Story's novel *The Condor's Shadow* I thought, "Whoa. Take a break**. You don't want this to be over so fast." My resolve lasted 20 seconds. **A ferocious current keeps pulling you along.**...

"People on the margins, in small towns, farms, ranches, seeking searching connecting not connecting....**This is a profound book**. [Jim Story's] grasp of social/psychological/political forces is subtle and far reaching. His knowledge of the physical world is vast. **And then there is the language, the pure magical brilliance of the language, that brings it all alive.**"

—Robert Roth, author *Health Proxy* and *Book of Pieces*

"Jim Story's *The Condor's Shadow* is **a captivating American odyssey**. It follows its fugitive protagonist's quest for meaning, from his hardscrabble youth to his apotheosis as a poet. Written with humor, grace and beauty, the ballad of Travis Mackey tells of his wanderings through the 20th Century agrarian west and northwest. It's **a fast-paced tale of a life lived well under difficult circumstances, a slice of Americana as delicious as your mother's homemade apple pie.**"

—Jonathan Woods, award-winning author of *Bad Juju, A Death in Mexico* and *Kiss the Devil Goodnight*

"**The Pacific Northwest comes alive in all its natural splendor** as the backdrop for this **poignant tale** about an enigmatic drifter who ambles in and out of sleepy no-where towns dodging trouble, but discovers **no matter how far he travels, his past is waiting in front of him.**"

—Eva Lesko Natiello, *New York Times* bestselling author of *The Memory Box* and *Following You*

"Jim Story again proves to be **a master storyteller**. In a deeply introspective tale…[and] a story of self-discovery, the novel is also a fine example of nature writing.…Another remarkable feature…is the focus on small-town America…specifically the rural communities of the Far West.…Though mindful of their frailties, he chooses instead to emphasize their humanity.… While focused on one segment of Americana, the novel **adds greatly to our understanding of the human condition.**"

—Manuel G. Gonzales, author of *Mexicanos: A History of Mexicans in the United States*

"*The Condor's Shadow*, Jim Story's new novel, **threads scenes like a Native American necklace, each skillfully worked bead different, yet bound together by a common theme**.... Will the California Condor of the Sierras, in its effortless flight high above, bring Travis his sought-for freedom from fear and guilt...? Read this **engrossing Odyssey through the American Northwest** to find the answer."

—Bob Bachner, author of *Last Clear Chance,*
Baby Grand, and *Killing Jack Armstrong*

"**Part mystery, part suspense with a dash of romance, this compelling, poignant, yet ultimately hopeful** novel tells the story of how a single violent event in a young man's life forces him, unfairly, to live his next eighteen years as a fugitive.... This **absorbing narrative** moves us back and forth in time and place, and like the Condor and the shadow it casts, the protagonist lives his life in relative solitude, always at a distance from those he hopes to connect with until fate ultimately leads him to a place of redemption, acceptance, and love."

—Cathie Borrie, author of *The Long Hello: Memory,*
My Mother, and Me

"Jim Story, deft author of the adventurous romp *Problems of Translation*, has given us another kind of journey. The rolling-stone hero of *The Condor's Shadow* is in constant flight from the violence of his past—until he is compelled and enabled to address it. This is **an engrossing story, cleverly woven—a hero's journey from an embattled youth to a hard-won maturity steeped in sorrow and acceptance.**"

—Hilary Orbach, author of *Transgressions and Other Stories*

"In **suspenseful, compelling** prose, Jim Story presents the tragic journey story of Clayton Poole, a man plagued by the memory of a youthful act of survival, the gravity of which ferments most acutely in his own conscience…. A brilliant illustration of **a moral man's battle with evil and his journey to recall his essential goodness.**"

—Stephanie Laterza, author of *The Psyche Trials*

"What a marvelous piece of work—**a genuine American saga** that sweeps us through history before we know it, and **a new take on the legend of the loner in the Great West** with **one of the most decent heroes in a long time**…. thoroughly masculine, but in a positive way. ….**Everyman in the way we would want him, and ourselves, to be,** even—maybe especially—in this current MeToo world."

—Ronald Story (no relation to Jim), author of *Jonathan Edwards and the Gospel of Love*

"a heart-wrenching tale that will appeal to audiences of all ages and interests…."

— Rachel Dehning, *Seattle Book Review*

THE CONDOR'S SHADOW

ALSO BY JIM STORY

PROBLEMS OF TRANSLATION
or
*Charlie's Comic, Terrifying, Romantic,
Loopy Round-the-World Journey
in Search of Linguistic Happiness*

THE CONDOR'S SHADOW

A NOVEL

JIM STORY

Blue Mile Books
New York, NY

Blue Mile Books, 2023.
Copyright © Jim C. Story, 2018.

All rights reserved by author. This includes the right to reproduce this book or portions thereof in any form whatsoever.

This is a work of fiction. Names, characters, places, and incidents are either the product of the author's imagination or used fictitiously. Any resemblance to actual persons, living or dead, events, or locales is entirely coincidental. An earlier version of Chapter 2 appeared as "Chasing the Condor" in The Same, 2011, Vol.8, No. 2. The two lines of the Spanish poem "Casida del Llanto" by Federico García Lorca, quoted in Chapter 4 and again in Chapter 6, are quoted by permission of Herederos de Federico García Lorca.

Library of Congress Cataloging-In-Publication Data
Names: Story, Jim, 1936- author.
Title: The condor's shadow : a novel / by Jim Story.
Description: [New York, New York] : Blue Mile Books, 2019.
Identifiers: ISBN 9780986238222 (paperback) |
    ISBN 9780986238239 (ebook)
Subjects: LCSH: Journalists--Montana--Fiction. | Identity
    (Psychology)--Fiction. | Self-realization--Fiction. | Life
    change events--Fiction. | Man-women relationships--
    Fiction. | Country life--West (U.S.)--Fiction.
Classification: LCC PS3619.T67 C66 2023 (print) | LCC
    PS3619.T67 (ebook) | DDC 813/.6--dc23

FIC000000 FICTION / General   FIC019000 FICTION / Literary
FIC066000 FICTION / Small Town & Rural

This book may be purchased in bulk for promotional, educational, or business use. Please contact your local bookseller or the publisher by email to *BlueMileBooks@gmail.com* .

Paperback ISBN: 978-0-9862382-2-2
eBook ISBN: 978-0-9862382-3-9

Library of Congress Control Number: 2023908777

For Jill

I have flown

west of Time and

south of Truth

    —From a poem by Clayton Poole

Contents

Prologue: Montana, 1971 1
Chapter 1: Southeast City, Washington, 1965 5
Chapter 2: California Coast Range, 1952 13
Chapter 3: Southeast City, Washington, 1965 35
Chapter 4: California, 1952-53 43
Chapter 5: Southeast City, Washington, 1965 57
Chapter 6: Arizona, Washington, Oregon, 1952-59 ... 63
Chapter 7: Southeast City, Washington, 1965 71
Chapter 8: Montana, 1970/71 77
Chapter 9: Southeast City, Washington, 1965 95
Chapter 10: Montana, 1970-71 101
Chapter 11: Southeast City, Washington, 1965 105
Chapter 12: Alaska, 1968 111
Chapter 13: Montana, 1970-71 123
Chapter 14: Montana 1970-71 135
Chapter 15: Montana 1970-71 145
Chapter 16: Montana 1970-71 153
Chapter 17: Southeast City, Washington, 1971 167
Chapter 18: Southeast City, Washington, 1971 177
Chapter 19: Southeast City, Washington, 1971 187
Chapter 20: California, 1971 195
Chapter 21: California, 1971 203
Chapter 22: California, 1971 211
Epilogue: Somewhere Outside Bend, Oregon, 2018 .. 223
Acknowledgments 233
Reading Group Guide 237
About the Author

Prologue

MONTANA, 1971

He felt the chill all the way down to his toes. Over many months, Clayton Poole, a thirty-four year old journalist working for The Rolling Hills Reporter in Montana, a young newspaper with a growing reputation, had become an avid reader of newspapers from other communities in the Pacific Northwest, all available to him in the paper's morgue. After all, he'd been to most of those places. Worked in most. While keen to keep a low profile, he'd nevertheless had small adventures in most.

Usually, he did this at night. It was a Sunday afternoon; nobody was around since the paper had come out the preceding day. As on other occasions, he took the keys to the morgue from the secretary's desk, unlocked the room behind the printing press, selected a few recent issues—more from places he'd been than places he'd not—and paged through, scanning for anything interesting. Pocatello was represented and Boise, as were Bellingham, Bozeman, Ellensburg, Corvallis, Klamath Falls, Coeur d'Alene, a few others.

But the one he never failed to check was Southeast City, Washington. And there in that community's *Union-Clarion*, as the summer of 1971 drew to a close, he discovered something that made the hairs on the back of his neck crawl. Tucked in among announcements about the Sweet Onion Festival, the awarding of the annual Kiwanis Club scholarships, and the issuing of new park rules by the city council, was a follow-up article on a shooting that had taken place a week earlier. A woman—name withheld—had admitted to the killing of her estranged husband—a former felon—and was in jail awaiting arraignment. The prosecutor had not yet decided what charges would be filed.

As he read on, Clayton's breath stopped. In its last paragraph, the story mentioned that the weapon used, a Savage Model 24 .22/.410, was unregistered and—so the woman claimed—had been left to her some years earlier by a person she refused to name. The newspaper, in a flamboyant touch, referred to this person as "the mysterious stranger."

The moment he finished reading Clayton rose to his feet involuntarily. He managed a few short, shallow breaths. "Holy shit!" he muttered. And again, "Holy shit!"

Hours later, after unbroken pacing and thinking in his room, Clayton called his editor, Frank Bascombe, and asked to meet him at the Iron Penny.

When the editor arrived he found Clayton in a booth, an empty brandy glass in front of him. After the two had ordered fresh drinks, Clayton cleared his throat and told Frank he needed to leave Rolling Hills immediately. When his boss probed him for a reason, he said only that something had come up elsewhere that demanded his immediate attention. He said he was sorry but he had no choice. He had to go.

The editor looked at him across the table, took a swallow of beer, rubbed his chin. Finally, he nodded and said, "You're him, aintcha."

For the second time that day, Clayton felt a cold wind pass through him. "What do you mean, Frank? I'm who?"

"The 'mysterious stranger.' You left the morgue files in a bit of disarray this afternoon. Very unlike you. So I scanned the newspaper and my eye settled on that story. That's how come you feel you need to leave. I'm damn sure of it. But what I don't know is why. Tell me, Clayton."

Clayton was silent, so the editor continued. "If you go, you'll be leaving a very good thing here, you know. You've worked your way into this community and become something of a linchpin, so to speak. We'd hate to see you go, Clayton. Hell, *I'd* hate to see you go! So please. Tell me. What it is that's goin' on. I figure you owe me that much."

At the editor's 'you owe me,' Clayton closed his eyes, slumped in his seat, shook his head slowly side to side. Then his head stopped, but his jaw moved back and forth. He opened his eyes, looked around the room to signal the barmaid for another brandy. He clasped his large hands around the side of his head, fingers loosely interlocked over his scalp. He closed his eyes again, tilted his head upward, rocked back and forth a time or two.

Across the table, Frank observed the struggle his newfound friend was going through. Looking at Clayton's anguished face now, he wondered: What in thunder could cause such consternation?

Clayton finally returned his attention to his friend and employer, looked him in the eyes. "You're right," he said. "I owe you. So here goes."

CHAPTER 1
SOUTHEAST CITY, WASHINGTON, 1965
MADDIE

When his cat, on her nightly run, streaked across the bottom of his bed, Rusty Thomas stirred, briefly. He heard the muffled thump of a nine-pound body slamming against a wooden roadblock but ignored it, changed position, dropped back into sleep. The cat, whose name was Burgundy, was habitually trying—and always failing—to make that leap to the top of the highboy. A few hours later, however, when Rusty awoke for good, he discovered this time had been different. Burgundy, instead of being curled up on the easy chair where he usually found her in the morning, lay alongside the piece of furniture which had been her nocturnal target, head fixed at an odd angle. Her body was already cold.

Rusty sank back onto the bed, His shoulders drooped. "Damn stupid cat!" he said finally. "Goddamn stubborn, stupid cat."

After he had drawn on his clothes and used the toilet, he wrapped Burgundy in an old tee shirt and hauled her outside to bury in the back yard. He selected a shovel from an assortment of tools propped against one wall of the small bungalow and chose a spot near the yellow roses. This house was a rental, but Mrs. Davidson had told him he had full leave to plant flowers or vegetables or whatever he wanted in his yard. He supposed that privilege extended to his cat.

After the burial he stood a moment, regarding the freshly turned and mounded earth with a blurry eye, before finally heaving a huge sigh. "Damned stupid cat!" he repeated. Then he returned indoors, this time to the living room (a constrained space whose dimensions were made even smaller by a looming gas stove the size of two ocean-going trunks—quiet now, since it was summertime), sat down on the edge of a formless old divan, and wept. He wept first for the cat, then for the state of the world in the Year of Our Lord 1965, which he valiantly tried to keep track of by a reasonably faithful parsing of newspapers and radio—he didn't own a television—and finally for his own miserable, roving, lonely life. A life that had grown noticeably darker now that Burgundy was gone.

He'd had one other cat during this haphazard,

hop-scotching life he'd led, when he'd worked way up north for a timber company. Actually that cat wasn't his to begin with; it had wandered into the bunkhouse where he stayed along with five other men and he was the only one to take care of it, so by default, it had become his. And it—she—did cozy up to him, purr for him, slept at the foot of his bed. He'd called her Alabaster, after her white, almost translucent fur. But she too met an untimely death, coming out second best in a tangle with a wolverine. So whether sheltered or roaming out of doors, it seemed his cats cultivated hazards by the bushel. But seriously, what were the chances that he'd own the only cat in existence to miscalculate a jump that badly? Perhaps Burgundy had suffered from dementia. Was that possible? In a cat?

That afternoon he climbed into his 1956 Ford pickup and drove north/northeast out along East Isaacs Avenue to Mill Creek Road and then east/southeast through the hills and ridges outside of town until he came to Meiner Road, where he turned left, wound back and forth a time or two before arriving at a natural turnout behind a huge old pine. He stopped, pulled on his emergency brake, and sat a moment. Below, a wide stream gurgled its way into a rare, quiet pool. Reaching for the binoculars he'd had since he was fifteen years old, he climbed out and moseyed downhill. Southeast City, in the corner of Washington State, was set near the Blue Mountains which, even these lower-lying ridges, were beautiful. They curled like knife-edges, occasionally flattening out to long stretches like wide loaves of bread, giving way again to humps and hillocks. And all along, interspersed among the rich grasses and rocky outcroppings, the hillsides erupted with pine, mountain ash, evergreen. Since it was summertime, birds flocked to these trees, particularly to the nuts dropped in cones by the pines, and flocked as well to the streams and rills that lay in the shadows of the ridges.

Hunkered down by the pool, the young man trained his binoculars on the tree branches. He spotted a flock of tree swallows first, common in these parts, their dark blue tops and white bodies blurring the air above the pond. Next he spied a Cassin's Finch, a little less common, a pretty male, with its vibrant red forehead and fading scarlet breast. Nuthatches and chickadees fluttered about nearby, chattering noisily. He didn't need the binoculars; he recognized the sounds. Still, he adjusted the glasses and watched them a moment, as they vied with the swallows for control of the pool. Was there anything as graceful as a flock of swallows? He heard something then, turned his head, trained his glasses at a distant evergreen. Dead tree, a skeleton, but still standing. Sure enough, there it was: a Pileated Woodpecker, drilling its way toward a new burrow. Well, that was a find.

He knew even more about birds at higher elevations, mostly those where he'd worked at logging. Especially condors, mainly in California, when he'd sought the highest elevations he could find. Only the last couple of years had he tried his luck here in Southeast City, working various jobs, reading books he'd checked out from the local library. He was tall, a slender young man, with broad shoulders, used to outdoor work. He'd worked the grain harvest around Southeast City, driving combines in the fields and later hauling wheat to the granaries, both jobs long familiar. Although he hadn't worked in the pea fields round about, he was nevertheless currently employed as a meter reader in the Libby, McNeill & Libby pea-canning plant on the northern edge of town. It was a mindless job—and certainly seasonal—but it would do until the middle of summer, when the whirring and clacking machines would fall silent and the doors would be bolted shut until the following year.

His time with the birds relaxed him. Driving towards home, he felt calmer, though the image of Burgundy leapfrogged through his mind from time to time.

Back on East Isaacs, he stopped for a cup of coffee at a diner he'd often thought of trying, a new spot just inside the city limits. Though he lived close to the heart of the town, near the college, he was customarily drawn to peripheries.

Inside, there was only one waitress, no other customers. He took a seat in a booth along the side. She approached him, coffee pot already in her hand.

"Cuppa?" she asked.

"You bet."

She filled his cup, retreated behind the counter and resumed swiping down its surface. As she was emptying the almost spent ketchup bottles into others, she looked up and noticed he'd finished his coffee and was still sitting there. She called out, "Another?"

"Please," he said.

"Why not come over to the counter, then, and keep me company while I work? Should it be that the last two people left on earth don't even talk to each other?"

He smiled, hauled himself out of the booth and brought his cup to the counter. "Fill me up, then."

While she continued to work, he looked at her. A few years older than he, perhaps. Thirty-one? Thirty-two? She had a slender, almost elfin build, but there was something tough about her. An edge. Dishwater blonde hair cut in a pageboy. Bangs draped over her forehead. Freckles across the bridge of her nose. Every once in a while she extended her lower lip and shot a column of air upwards, such that her fluttering bangs disclosed somewhat lighter eyebrows. Some old injury had left a scar along her hairline, he noticed. Her eyes were small and dark, merry one moment, wary the next. Or probing, could be. In fact, he began to see her eyes as loaded like a shotgun, ready to explode into a thousand meanings, a fire-fall of moods. As he continued to regard her, some thought or memory relaxed her dark lips into a smile that opened her face as if it had suddenly been turned toward the sun.

Amused by his gaze, she arrested her work to stare back, one hand on an outthrust hip, apron jiggling slightly from a tapping foot.

"Hey," he said suddenly, "I just won a contest. On the radio? They called and asked a question that I answered correctly…"

"Congratulations."

"No, what I mean is, they sent me a lot of merchandise I can't use. Stuff from local stores? Promotion, I guess. So, you have any use for…" He hesitated, looked away, looked back. "…a pair of medium-length taupe nylons?"

She was quiet for half a beat, then responded, "What was the question?"

She had a nice voice, he decided. Pitched low, but syrupy, somehow. Warm.

"Excuse me? Oh, the one I answered, you mean. They asked did I know who was the first American into space. And I did. Alan Shepard."

She studied him then, as if toggling between two choices in a hand of poker. Finally, she grinned. She stepped back, lifted her skirt a few inches. "Matter of fact, I do," she said.

There was a run in one of her stockings, extending from mid-thigh on down.

"Yes," he said. "I see."

After the hem of her uniform had dropped down like a curtain, he cleared his throat and looked away a moment. "Well," he said, "there you are then."

Without another word, he exited the café, went to his pickup, and returned with a glossy package.

———————

The Iron Penny, with its usual ebb and flow of customers, had picked up a few over the last hour, but now the crowd was beginning to thin out again.

Clayton sought his editor's eyes across the booth. "Not going to be enough, is it, Frank?"

"Not really, I'm afraid."

"Okay, then. Let me start at the beginning."

Chapter 2

CALIFORNIA COAST RANGE, 1952

Travis

1. Pa

The late October sun on his eyelids made him think of freshly baked bread, which he'd not had any of since his mama died. It was Saturday. Having completed his homework and washed and polished the car, fifteen-year-old Travis Mackey wandered about the mine behind his house. This was his alone time.

Near the mine's maw he found his clump of neatly arranged small rocks and hunkered down against a broad gate of wooden planks. The apparatus dwarfed him, resembling a large sluice stretching behind him up the hillside, but what the gate restrained was a small glacier of white powder. Where he now stood, trucks had once backed up to be loaded with the hillside's freshly excavated treasure: gypsum.

Travis examined his small pile of rocks, stroking them, rearranging them. They were fragments he had gathered, over time, from different parts of the property. Quartz crystals, selenite, chert. Elements as familiar to him as different trees and bushes to someone growing up in a forest. Alabaster. Satin spar. Pure gypsum—that which got transformed into chalk, or plaster casts—was so soft you could scratch it with your fingernail. What remained at this site was mainly gypsite: tiny gypsum crystals mixed with clay and sand. Most of the heavy machinery had long since been removed. What was left was gypsite and scattered mineral fragments: these rocks. These were his playthings, his treasures. His friends.

Distractedly, he turned these chunks over in his palm, rubbed them gently against one another, finally drew designs in the sand, like images caught in a kaleidoscope.

As he fiddled, he was remembering what had happened the previous day, in biology class. A girl had looked at him. Travis was fifteen, a sophomore at his high school. Yesterday, a girl had looked at him and it had warmed him. Once, at another mine site, Travis had stared into a shaft he'd been told was a mile deep. He remembered his sensations at that moment. Standing on the rim of that hole had made him giddy. He'd an impulse to jump, yet was afraid to jump; there was the sense he might throw himself in, without actually willing it to happen. The dark brown eyes of this girl had made him feel the same way.

Her name was Imogene. She sat in the first row, but she had turned around, and looked at him. He hadn't been able to unlock himself from her eyes until she'd faced the front again.

Sighing, he returned the rocks to their corner place near the chute. Stretching to his full height, five ten or thereabouts, he clambered up the side of the twelve-foot wooden gate and jumped off into the loose hill of powder on the other side.

Knee-deep in gypsite dust, he struggled up the hill toward its source: the hammer mill where the gypsum rocks were ground, and the old, dead wheel itself. A small cabin stood alongside, where an operator had once kept this machinery—the only equipment left on the hillside—humming. Though all gasoline had long ago been drained from the engine, Travis enjoyed maneuvering the big levers anyway. He yanked one, then the other, visualizing the huge wheel turning, to great noise, imagining the rock powerless before the force he controlled with his hands. After a few minutes, tiring of this, he found another stash of crystals that he'd hoarded in a corner of the cabin and launched them into one another over the wooden floor as one might play shuffleboard, or bocce ball. These particular crystals he had spent some time, on earlier days, grinding against each other or against the dead engine, until they were round enough to roll more easily across the floor.

At length, darkness began to fall. Reluctantly, Travis

left the mine and walked toward the house, entering as quietly as he could, remembering—too late—to catch the door before it banged.

"Damn you, boy!" shouted his father, rousing himself from the rocking chair in the living room. All lengthy angles, the man unfolded like a giant Praying Mantis. With his wild gray hair and knobby hands, he was a terrifying sight. Every Saturday he occupied this spot, angled toward the window and the mine, a silver-framed picture of the boy's mother beside him on a small table, alongside a glass and a half-full bottle of whiskey.

"What you trying to do to me, boy? I warned you about such racket! Stupid bastard!"

The boy held his breath. It was always something. A slammed door. A smudge on a drinking glass. Too much time spent washing the Essex, or not enough. Saturday afternoon was the only time his father drank now. But always with the same outcome: he would finger her photograph and stare out the window, drinking, until...

"Please, papa..."

"Don't you *pleasepapa* me, you smartass! I'll teach you what's what. Bring me my goddamned razor strop!"

Exhaling softly—hesitating only a moment—Travis entered the old man's bedroom, reached behind the door for the hanging nail, and returned with the strop.

Silently he unbuckled his belt, lowered his underpants, and bent over to grip his ankles.

The first blow, on his legs, sent waves of pain rocketing along his spine. He opened his mouth to a sudden, spontaneous breath, then clenched his teeth for the second jolt.

Eight blows later he began to cry, but silently. Tears filled his throat, his nostrils, almost choking him, but somehow he kept from screaming and the tears dripped off his face onto the floor. Somewhere past a dozen he lost count; he trembled but was blessedly numb.

Finally, it was over. Swallowing the mucus in his nose and throat, the boy pulled up his pants, wincing when the cloth touched his skin but knowing that he needed to move quickly to ward off further punishment.

The old man sank exhausted into the rocking chair. Breathing heavily, he threw back his whiskey and poured himself another glass.

Travis retrieved the discarded razor strop and returned it to its place, then stumbled into his own room, peeling off his britches and lying on his stomach. He was still breathing unevenly, but he tried to keep his struggle silent. When he'd reached the familiar stage where his buttocks and thighs felt like roasting strips of meat, he turned his face toward the wall and stared at a nail hole where a picture had once hung. *That was the last time, old man*, he said to himself. *Absolutely the last.*

2. The Condor

TRAVIS' father was caretaker of the Foothills Mine, a shut-down site in the Coast Range in California. Five years earlier Travis's mother had died and then, after a mining accident had reduced the old man's usefulness—following a career spent in several different locations as the parent company, Forrester Mines, shifted its workers as its priorities shifted, from one site to another—two years ago the company had installed the man and his boy here. The spot had been abandoned because it was no longer profitable to invest men and equipment in carrying away the meager reserves that remained of the mineral they mined. But you never knew when someone might find a use for what was left behind, and the company didn't want every man and his brother wandering up to try his luck. No heroics required, they assured him. "Your presence should be enough."

Father and son lived alone and had only a little need for what came from stores. Flour, lard, salt. Petrol for the vehicles, kerosene for the lamps. Matches and cartridges were also important, as was the occasional case of booze for the old man. The father hunted small game with a varmint gun, a Savage Model 24 over-under .22/.410, one part small-charge shotgun, one part small-bore rifle. An unlikely weapon for scaring off poachers, perhaps, had there been any. But useful for rabbit and squirrel, or the occasional covey of quail. Out back was a vegetable garden, where the old man spent a lot of time. Water came to the sink, though the privy was outdoors. They bought milk and eggs from a childless trapper and his wife who lived even further back in the hills. For other provisions, and the old man's meager monthly check, they would drive west, over the pass, to Salinas. If you drove the other way, down into the valley, it was forty miles to the small agricultural community known as Tule.

Tule was where the boy went to school. But the Tule Union High School bus route stretched only as far as the edge of the Central Valley's westernmost ranch, on Panoche Road, five miles before the hills leading up to this property even began.

So Travis drove down to meet the bus. Every morning. He was only fifteen, but he'd driven since he was twelve. The car he used was a 1928 Essex, which he parked in the shadow of the grain elevator, a hundred yards from the ranch's company store. School kids were sure to gawk and ask questions about a stately, twenty-two year-old Essex, and Travis was reluctant to explain to his peers how it had come into his possession. Plus he hoped to avoid questions from authorities as to whether he had a license, which he did not.

The bus driver had agreed to wait five minutes if he wasn't there on time. But on the Monday after that Saturday in October, he'd driven less than half a mile past the gate that closed off the company property when his peripheral vision caught something unusual. He slowed and stopped.

From this distance, it was only a black speck. But given that the colors of the surrounding countryside were either washed-out brown or the bleached grey-green of tumbleweeds, it was like seeing a painting on which someone had daubed a tiny black dot.

Travis reached inside the glove compartment for the binoculars. Powerful binoculars. They belonged to the company. Normally they were kept in his pa's pickup. But he'd borrowed them a while back and the old man had never noticed they were gone.

As soon as he adjusted the glasses, his heart stopped. He swallowed, pulled the glasses away from his eyes a moment, then brought them up and looked again.

The class he shared with Imogene was biology and because of their teacher's passion, they'd already spent a lot of time on birds. Travis had seen photographs of Hawk-Headed Parrots from Brazil, Madagascar Red Owls, hummingbirds, peacocks, and, most intriguing of all to the boy: *gymnogyps californianus*, the California Condor. *Right here in California*, the teacher had told them, *is the most amazing bird of all. Kin to both the vulture and the hawk, it presides over all, soaring among the peaks of the Coast Range, riding the updrafts on its ten-foot wingspan. A survivor from the Pleistocene. None could fly higher*, he insisted, *nor soar longer without flapping its wings. It glides along lofty snow-capped ridges and soars above hollowed-out ravines, looking for something dead.*

Travis drew down his binoculars a moment. A condor in his own back yard? He raised the glasses again. As he watched, the bird unfolded its wings, stretched its head around in a circle, its stubby, down-turned beak leading the way, then re-folded the wings. Shit! The King of Birds. It could go anywhere it wanted, but it came here.

Could he get closer? He eased the car into gear and drove slowly off the road. There was a small embankment he had to descend before reaching the broad mesa, which undulated unevenly like the swells of a disturbed sea, strewn with scattered rocks, pockets of pure sand, badger holes. He knew he needed to choose his route with care. Tumbleweeds could wrap around the spokes of the wheels.

After two hundred yards he stopped. The bird hadn't moved. He groped on the seat for the binoculars.

Persimmon-colored head. Red muff with a coal-black fringe of puffy, stringy feathers, feathers so fine you could probably thread them through a needle. It was a condor all right. No question.

He eased himself out of the car and began to pick his way forward carefully, not wanting to step in a badger hole and stumble. A tension, brittle as broom-straw, filled his body.

He closed to within thirty paces before the bird began to rise, at first heading away, then circling: a long, slow ascending arc. Back toward the high country. When it was a hundred yards high or more, he wondered, what could it see? The gypsum mine? His house even? Soon it would see…what? His school? The Pacific? All of California?

He imagined that from where it now flew it could already pick out his father, puttering among the okra and tomatoes. Why, it could easily dive on his father like the predatory creature it was! Could plummet down, with blinding speed, until it plucked the old man from his garden, seizing and squeezing until its razor-sharp talons punctured his body and, when he was dead, rip flesh from bone with its beak.

Alone on the mesa, Travis shuddered and looked down at the ground. Then he shook his head to clear it and walked back to the car.

Returning to the county road, he drove west instead of east now, past the turnoff to the mine. Long before he reached Salinas, however, he veered left onto a graveled side road that reached into higher country, until he came to a little road he knew, which ran alongside a small brook curving back into the hills. Scattered trees began to appear, finally a meadow covered with tall grasses and wildflowers, mostly golden California poppies. He stopped. He'd been here before.

He stretched out in the back seat of the Essex, with all the doors closed, feeling warm and protected. A condor. Damn. A condor.

He fell asleep awhile, then awoke, ate the sandwich and cucumber he had brought with him for school, gathered pebbles along the stream bed and tossed them at clumps of grass, or branches of trees.

Mostly, he sat on the running board, in the shade of the car, and thought. The car was a comfort to him. Like the rocks, it was a friend.

He knew the story, from endless retellings.

His father had won the Essex in a poker game. Luck had been with him all evening, and a heavy-set Tehachapi barkeep they called Two Bits—the only non-miner in the game—had been anxious to recoup his losses. So when Two Bits finally drew a second pair, and held both Kings and Queens, he was willing to bet big. He bet the car. When the boy's father took a sip of whiskey and calmly laid down Ace, King, Queen, Jack, Ten—all Hearts—the whole table hushed. For almost a minute old Two Bits sat there with his eyes closed, then shoved his chair back and stood up, reaching into the pot to clasp the keys, tossing them to the boy's father himself. Then he stormed out, weaving a web of oaths around him as he went.

Travis's mother hadn't liked his father's drinking or his cards, but when he brought home that automobile, all was forgiven. She felt like a queen being ferried around in a coach-and-four when they went downtown. That was how the story went. Like a queen. And his father had been happy then. So he claimed.

His father stopped playing poker, fearful that he'd lose back the only thing of substance he had ever owned. And the grand old car became their good luck charm, a flashy symbol of fortune's turn in their direction.

But then, as Travis knew well, fortune swerved away again. Returning from a party one moonless night, they struck a rogue rock. Or so his father said. The car lurched sharply, the door swung open and Travis' mother, rummaging in the back seat for a blanket, was hurled onto the shoulder. Her neck "snapped like a twig."

Travis was ten when this happened. Afterwards, everything changed. Everything. His father grew morose. Always a quiet man, he hardly spoke at all now. He swore the car was a coffin, and refused to drive it. He hitched rides with co-workers to the Tehachapi Mine, or the Death Valley mine, wherever they were. Still, it was their only car. Travis, who couldn't see his mother's death as the car's fault, begged his father for lessons. The disgruntled man instructed Travis on two ventures down a very straight road in Death Valley, then stopped abruptly. Travis, however, pinched the keys and practiced on his own.

Then came the scraper accident. Travis' father was in the hospital for months, while the union paid the bills and Travis learned to drive in earnest. When the old man was discharged from the hospital and the company reassigned him, they threw in a pickup to haul supplies with, and that was what he drove from that day forward.

So Travis inherited the car, built eight years before he was born. It still had original upholstery. He washed and polished it once a week, smiling at how the azure color returned once the Valley dust was wiped away, loving how he could buff the spokes of its chrome wheels to a perfect shine.

There was, of course, no way caring for the car could bring back his mother, but it helped him remember her. A small woman, with large hazel eyes and a boundless energy, she buzzed through the day cleaning and dusting, darning and knitting, or putting up jams and jellies to last through the winter. But she always had time for Travis, time to help him with his sums or his reading, for unlike her husband she had finished high school, and with honors. And while she did not interfere with his father's disciplining him when they both agreed he'd misbehaved, she guarded the boy fiercely when the old man was into his cups and simply needed something to lash out at, bodily shielding Travis and daring the old man to hit her instead, which he would never, ever do. These days Travis carried around inside him an emptiness he could not name. And now the beatings had become routine, as predictable as the ticking of a clock.

3. *The Stranger*

THE following Saturday was shrouded. All morning rain had approached, hovered and retreated, clouds drifting in over the barren, rocky Coast Range from the Pacific. Noon found Travis reading a book he'd borrowed from the school library, a book recommended by Imogene. Her favorite, she said. His father was gone and, in fact, overdue, having driven into Salinas that morning. When he returned there would be plenty to unload. He hoped the old man had remembered to throw a tarp across the provisions so they wouldn't get wet.

Finishing the story, he put the book aside. Everything seemed to be about birds now! The story told of a falcon trained by a teenage boy in Wyoming. It would hunt on command, then return to perch on the boy's leather-encased forearm. He smiled. Imagine having a condor perch on your arm. For that matter, imagine Imogene on your arm. Or in your arms! Over the last several days he had actually stood close to her a time or two, close enough to feel the warmth from her body, to smell her breath, fragrant from the small mints she chewed. He had talked to her in the school cafeteria, and sitting on the steps outside the main building after school, her trim legs dangling off the concrete balustrade.

Suddenly a car door slammed and Travis frowned. It didn't sound like the pickup. He went to the window and looked out.

A pickup, all right, but not his pa's. A big one, outfitted with powerful-looking dual spotlights. Shiny and new, though mud encrusted the underside and clung to the bottom edge of the cab.

Next to the cab stood a short, hatless stranger. He appeared to be taking stock of the property. He was casually dressed, and something about his face alarmed the boy; it had the sag and spread of an overripe cantaloupe. His hair was patchy, as if someone had taken a pot of paste and stuck tufts of cat hair randomly around his head. When he turned briefly toward the house, the boy could see a plastic shirt-pocket guard stuffed with mechanical pens. But what he noticed next was alarming. On his hip was a gun, but no sign of a badge.

The man started for the house, but abruptly changed his mind and began to circle around the front of the mine, making for the chutes where Travis kept his hoard of rocks. Travis turned from the window. His heart beat fast. The man was trespassing, but Pa wasn't here. Weren't they supposed to scare him off?

Almost without thinking, he went into his pa's bedroom and lifted the varmint gun from its rack on the wall. On a nearby shelf were both shotgun and rifle cartridges. He loaded the top chamber with a .410 shell filled with double-ought buckshot; into the bottom chamber he slipped a .22-short hollow-point. Then he found his yellow rain-slicker and shrugged it on. He would try to be cool. If he held the gun down along his body under the slicker, it wouldn't be noticed. He practiced a few times to see if he could raise the gun through the opening of the slicker quickly enough. Before he left the house he dropped a few more shells of each kind into the pocket of his slicker. He planned to be polite, but he wanted to be prepared.

Closing the front door quietly, Travis walked to where the man had disappeared around the bend of the mine. He spotted him there, hunkered down, absorbed in the pile of crystals the boy had nested against the wooden chute. When Travis was about ten yards away, the man heard the crunch of gravel and startled, then rose slowly and turned around.

"Hey," he said. "You must be the boy."

Fear flickered through Travis, a small wind looking for the hollow places. *You must be the boy?*

"Name's Callahan. Knew your father. Said the two of you live here alone."

Travis' heart beat wildly. Why would his father tell him that? Where was his pa now?

The man cast his eyes around a moment, up the hill and back.

"Dressed for rain, are ye?" He grinned. "Wal, you might be right at that." He stuck his hand out as a few drops began to fall, a light mist settling across his upturned palm. He ran his hand through the little grass islands on his head.

"This mine's still got lotsa good gypsite, you know that, boy? They should nevera closed it."

The boy spoke at last. "Belongs to the Clayton Company. We're just up here to keep out trespassers."

The man laughed then, a short, quick bark. "Oh, ye are, are ye? Wal, good for you. Keep out the damned trespassers. Like me, ya mean."

Travis said nothing.

"Lemme tell ya somethin', boy. You know where your Pa is now? Your precious Pa? You'll never see him again, that's for sure. He was mouthin' off about this mine in a store in Salinas, where I seen him grubbin' up. He was the one admitted there was still good stuff here. It interested me."

He took a step forward, then stopped. Travis, tensing, could feel the gun's stock against his ribs.

"I followed him, run him to ground up on the ridge. Once I got him stopped, I tried to talk some sense into him about doin' a little minin' of our own. A partnership. Flat out fifty-fifty deal. Stupid old cocksucker wouldn't bite!"

He stopped and grinned at the boy.

"What do you think of that, boy? Man don't want to go partners, so I figure I'll have to do it by myself, if he was right about the mine. But then he tells me about his young, strong, good-lookin' boy, and I think, now, there's the ticket. Get the boy to work some. Me work some. Hell, we can make us some money and have us some fun at the same time. Am I right?"

The man who'd called himself Callahan licked his lips. "Am I right, boy? Healthy young buck like you, you like to have fun, don'tcha?" The man leaned in.

"Where's my pa?" The boy blurted it out, though he was careful not to move when he did so.

"Wal, him and me had a little argument, ya see? Didn't

see eye to eye on this business. So I had to take extreme measures. Know what that means? 'Extreme measures'?"

Travis knew what he meant it to mean, but did he believe him?

"Your dad and his pickup are in a place they'll never be found, boy. Never. I had no choice. They'll never find 'im. Never. Cantankerous old fart that he was, I doubt it's much of a loss."

Travis felt the need to swallow but had no spit. What the man said must be true. Else, where was his Pa? He could feel his jaw twitching, hoped the man couldn't see. The man was no longer smiling.

"So you can just go fuck your precious Clayton Company, you hear me? This mine belongs to me now. And since you're such a young cunt, I'm gonna let you live. Mebbe. If you do as I say. So why don't you just go back to the house there, and relax, sonny. You're dad is dead. You and me are gonna work this mine and have us some fun into the bargain. You belong to me now, hook line and sinker. You get me, boy?"

A heartbeat or two may have passed after the man's last words, but later, Travis couldn't remember. He poked the gun through the opening in his slicker and unloaded both barrels. What he did remember was the look of surprise on the man's face just before he collapsed.

"Oh, shit!" muttered the man. "Oh, shit, it hurts." He was struggling, very slowly, to get at the gun in his holster, but the boy quickly dropped another .410 shell in the chamber and blew apart the hand that was reaching. The man shuddered, and stared straight ahead as the boy approached and stood over him.

"Goddamn you," he whispered. "Goddamn you to hell. You gotta help me, boy. They's doctors in town. Gotta find me a doctor. This…ain't…right. I'm hurt real bad. Gotta…."

The man passed out. There were two badly bleeding wounds in his torso, one in the abdomen and another in the chest, where the hollow-point had scooped out a three-inch hole near the clavicle. The boy stood over him a moment, watching him bleed, then looked around, not knowing what to do—shoot him again or go for a doctor, like the man said. A fine rain was falling fast now.

Laying his gun aside, Travis seized the man's good arm and dragged him, with great difficulty, closer to the chute gate. Next he scooped up his rocks from where the man had been examining them and moved them and his shotgun safely out of the way. He climbed the gate until he reached the lever that opened it. It was stuck; he had to strain and pound with doubled fists to make it budge, but at last it was open enough. Pouring through the gate, white powder gradually covered the body. When it was done, he closed it and climbed down.

He picked up the gun, and stood thinking a few moments, leaning against the wooden restraints. Then he collected his crystals, distributing them between the two pockets of his rain slicker. No sooner had he done so, however, than he began to think again. He took the crystals out of his pocket and looked at them. Then, one by one, he tossed them up into the powder behind the sluice gates.

Inside the house, he moved quickly and methodically. He stripped off the slicker, tossing it onto his pa's rocker. He lifted a loose floorboard under a chenille rug in the old man's bedroom and from that dark pocket withdrew a cookie tin. He counted the money. Over two hundred dollars in small bills. Stuffing the bills into his shirt pocket, he tossed the tin back in the hole, replaced the floorboard, spread the rug over it.

In his own room he grabbed jeans and shirts from his closet, rummaged through a drawer for socks and shorts. There were paper sacks in the kitchen, and he returned with a big one to stuff the clothing into. He picked up the bag, returned to the living room, lifted his slicker off the rocker. He patted his pants pocket to assure himself he had the car keys, then his shirt pocket for the money.

It took him an hour to dispose of the pickup. There was a long, slow curve about a quarter mile from the house toward the county road, giving way on the inside to a deep ravine. The road sloped sideways downward toward the gully, and, after driving it there and positioning it carefully, the boy was able to disengage the gears and push the pickup into the gulch without trouble. It clattered and bounded down the mountainside, quickly becoming lost in the underbrush. He wiped out the tire tracks with a tumbleweed and walked back.

Outside the cabin once more, he stood and thought a moment. Then he reentered the house, took his mother's picture from the table beside the rocking chair, and left. He strode to the Essex with a light step now, through the gentle drizzle. He laid his possessions beside him on the seat.

When he reached the county road he stopped the car and stepped out a minute to adjust a stuck windshield wiper. To the right lay the Valley, the high school, Imogene. To the left lay Salinas, and the high peaks of the Coast Range. In that direction, he could see a break in the clouds; the sun would soon be out. When he returned to the driver's seat he sat quietly a moment, then put the car in gear and turned left. There was no one around to hear the soft crunch of gravel or see the car move smoothly up the road through the misty rain.

Chapter 3

SOUTHEAST CITY, WASHINGTON, 1965

Maddie

Rusty stood alongside the last of eight production lines where tops got stamped onto cans of peas, clipboard and pencil held lightly at his side. He realized for the first time that motes of dust he could see in the shaft of sunlight streaming through the factory door—thousands of tiny particles, millions, perhaps—must be settling in the cans as well, a tiny sprinkle of Southeast City seasoning just before each can gets a top slapped on, trapping the motes forever. Or until it is opened by an unsuspecting housewife a month, a year, or several years from this moment.

He allowed himself a small frown.

"Don't worry about it none," urged a gravelly voice beside him. A man as wide as a highway, who wore a foreman's cap and chewed a sizeable wad of gum with his mouth open, lumbered up beside him. His name, Rusty knew, was Hanratty. "I know what you're thinking," said Hanratty, "but it's okay. Those bins there"—he gestured toward the squat openwork iron cylinders on rollers, into which the cans tumbled as they came off the conveyor belt—"get rolled right over to the cook-pit, where the water boils 'em for an hour before they're taken out, dried, labeled and packed for shipment. Ain't nothin' in there gonna harm anybody after that."

"Umm," said Rusty. "That's good." Kills all the germs, he was thinking. But don't water and dust make mud? There's a surprise for the happy homemaker!

"Say, Rusty," Hanratty said, "gonna give you a heads-up. I know writin' down what the meters say every fifteen minutes takes about five or so to do. It's important work. It's our record keeping. How many cans of what type, etc. But I can't say it keeps you overly busy. Now. On Saturday they's an efficiency expert coming up from our headquarters in San Francisco, and, lemme tell ya, he's lookin' to cut jobs. So in between taking your readings, you best wander the plant a little bit and look busy, or head off into the shipping room out of sight when you spot this guy runnin' around the plant with a broom up his ass. Ya get me?"

Rusty nodded. "Thanks, Hanny. I'll remember."

Two customers held places at the counter when Rusty walked into the Tip Top Diner the following Sunday. A family of four occupied a booth against the wall. Madelyn Badger, the waitress to whom he'd bequeathed the nylons on his previous visit, smiled and whispered something to the short-order cook. Joaquin, a tall, sleepy-looking fellow in a soiled apron, turned a flapjack, then glanced sideways at Rusty. A mess of ink-black hair straggled out from under his Southeast City Little League baseball cap. He shrugged, made an indifferent arc with his spatula, returned to the grill. Madelyn tossed her head toward the back of the restaurant and Rusty followed her through the kitchen, along a corridor, and out a side door.

"How ya been?" she asked, patting the set of concrete steps just outside the screen door, inviting him to sit. "Getting worried I wouldn't see you again."

"Busy with my job is all. How's them nylons working out?"

Her eyes danced. "Still in their package. Saving them for a special occasion."

They became quiet, staring at the graveled roadbed of the alleyway. Rusty's restive mind swelled with information about what he was looking at, like a sponge soaking up whatever water was available. He was looking at the gravel. *Limestone*, he thought. *Trace of quartzite.* A flock of sparrows, chattering like women at a quilting bee, fluttered nearby.

She reached under her apron, pulled out a pack of Luckys. She extended the pack toward him. "Smoke?"

"No thanks. Gave it up."

She lit up, took a deep drag. After exhaling, she stared at the nozzle of her cigarette, rolled it back and forth in her fingers a time or two. "How long did you smoke?"

"Decade or so, I guess." He struggled with himself a moment, unsure how his next thought would be heard. Thinking bold, but feeling shy. Or not wanting to queer things with an attractive woman. "Bad for your health, though. I read the Surgeon General says so. Fact, it may be right there on your cigarette pack."

She studied the warning on the label a moment. Then she drew back and examined him as carefully as she had the cigarettes. "Never noticed that."

"Best if you'd give it up too. Might live longer."

"Life gave me some better perks, I might consider that."

"I hear you, but it's all we've got, isn't it."

She looked at her cigarette again, twirled it around in her fingers as if inspecting an apple for soft spots. "Y'know, you're right."

Standing, she flipped the butt out onto the roadway. A dumpster was parked behind the restaurant, and she tossed the cigarette pack into it.

"And tonight? I'm gonna gargle with Listerine for half an hour."

He grinned. "Might be excessive. Two minutes is prob'ly enough."

She flounced down beside him once again, tucked her arm inside his. After a moment, she lay her head against his shoulder. "My protector."

"If you say so." He slipped an arm around her waist. "Actually, I just read a lot."

The main factory room was huge, with empty cans barreling around three sides at the very top, sandwiched securely enough between four wide rubber bands moving at a constant rate. The clatter they made as they streaked along was huge and for the most part their voyage was smooth, if noisy. But every once in a while, a can that was malformed or hadn't made it properly onto the runway would send the whole clattering assembly line into cardiac arrest. Rusty had seen seasoned veterans of the pea-canning staff seize a flexible birch stick about twice the length of a vaulting pole, and poke out the offending can so the rest could resume their run. This Saturday, remembering Hanratty's warning, he'd begun lugging one of the long poles around the factory floor between meter reading, wearing an expression suggesting that—were it not for his vigilance—the whole plant would be forced to shut down any minute. He thought he looked a comical sight but, in the interests of keeping his job, he was willing to do it.

Still, he preferred his alternative ruse, which was

to disappear into the shipping room for a ten-minute interval between readings. How many years now since he'd discovered that he enjoyed writing poetry? That was why he'd moved to Southeast City. To be near the college. Through a program called Town and Gown Initiative, he'd spent many happy hours in the library's reading room. The librarian, a tall Eastern European lady of fifty or so, with granny glasses and a smile that began slow and grew until it took up her whole face, had become his friend and mentor. Mrs. Skorecky had informed him of another program that enabled town folk to "sit in" on particular courses at the college, and he'd made plans to try a writing seminar in the fall.

During the moments he spent in the shipping room, he'd try to write poems, more or less imitating what he was reading. Most were about birds, several featuring the California Condor he'd seen up close, once, years ago. But just now he wasn't thinking about birds. He was thinking about a man from his past who wore a pocket-protector full of pens and carried a pistol he never got to use.

On the side of a container of Number Eight peas, he wrote:

We seek control.

He paused, then resumed:

We seek it with guns.
We seek it with a steely gaze
      or with muscle and heft,
With a huge surrounding, a menacing glance.

Or we seek it with elections, posters,
    promises,
        lies and illusions.
We seek it with guns.

Just then, he checked his watch and scurried back through the plant to Line Number One. He'd need to fudge his timekeeping sheet by a minute or two.

Chapter 4
CALIFORNIA, 1952-53
Alejandro

Curve after curve, the ice-blue Essex kicking up dust or humming along the tarmac, Travis was convinced all roads lay upward. Until they didn't.

Following the cue of the condor he'd seen less than a week ago, his only inclination was to climb. But he soon discovered that the side roads snaking around the hills of the California Coast Range, though their initial upwards incline might suggest a higher elevation, seldom delivered on that promise. Sooner or later each dirt road had to be abandoned, so he'd retrace his path to the asphalt and try again at the next one.

Eventually he abandoned this strategy altogether and began to look at maps. On the main roads, he could refuel, grab some snacks, use the restroom, and buy another map, which he would consult at the very next turnout. A few proprietors regarded him warily. Because of his youth, he supposed, or maybe they were taken aback by the handsome touring car visible through their picture window—nearly a quarter of a century old—but he never invited conversation, and asked directions from no one. He remained in a state of high alert and capacious nervous energy, but each stop reminded him that the $200 wad of small bills he'd taken from his father's savings beneath the floorboard would not last forever.

He continued all night, munching when hungry on potato chips and peanuts, *Baby Ruths* and *Crackerjacks*, *Big Hunks* and *Fritos*. Candy bars were five cents each. He bought a six-pack of Royal Crown Cola (thirty-five cents), which he sipped from time to time. One filling station offered a wrapped baloney sandwich for forty cents which he snapped up, only to toss it a few minutes later when he unwrapped it to discover a smell like dead possum. He hoped the squirrels and the birds had better stomachs than he did. Twice he pulled over to well-hidden turnouts and slept for an hour or two, then woke up and pressed on. The Essex performed beautifully and he drove with care. Not only did he love this car, he needed it to last forever.

The air grew thinner and the trees bigger. He realized he was among redwoods. Shortly after eight a.m. of the second day, he came across a small town called Sequoiaville. He'd spotted it on the map; it was near Ray's Peak, the highest elevation he'd discovered in these mountains, not too far south of San Francisco. Around the first bend, about 200 yards past the "Welcome" sign (population at 2,341), he encountered the Skyline Motel-Lodge, a modest-looking place with gasoline pumps out front, a diner, and a graveled parking area, around which six small bungalows clustered, their white paint peeling. At the moment, no cars were parked beside the units, but one battered-looking truck stood guard outside the restaurant. A large, painted wooden sign read: "Where the Trees Are." A neon sign blinked: *Vacancies*. An old *Schwinn* bicycle leaned against the wall of the café.

Travis brought the Essex to a stop in the middle of the road and thought a minute. "This is it," he said aloud. Then, more quietly, "This is where I'm going to be for awhile." He pulled up beside the truck.

A man in slightly soiled kitchen whites turned out to be the owner of the motel/café. He seemed glad to see him. Almost as if he'd been waiting for him. He served Travis a huge breakfast on the house, and after just a few spare minutes of questions, he offered the boy a job on the spot, for seventy-five cents an hour. A big fellow who wore overalls and a gray sweatshirt underneath his kitchen garb and looked to be in his middle fifties, he called himself Hercule Poitier and claimed to be French, though he pronounce it "Her-cool Poyteer" and had no trace of a French accent Travis could detect. When asked about his age, Travis said he was eighteen and the man nodded his head slowly. Was that an amused flicker of doubt in the man's eyes?

"I need somebody to do sweeping up and dishwashing," said Mr. Poyteer. "Plus cleaning the motel rooms after people leave. Can you handle that?"

Travis nodded.

"Well, then," said the man. "It's settled. You'll share duties with the other boy."

The other boy?

The very next morning Poitier asked if he had any ID. Travis looked down at the floor, at the wall, at the ceiling. He shook his head. "I do not, sir."

"Well, sometimes state inspectors drop by. If they do, you'll need ID. You said your name was Skate?"

"Yes sir. Skate McHenry."

Travis had no idea why he'd called himself Skate. It had just popped out. On the other hand, there'd been a family at the Tehachapi mines whose last name was McHenry.

"Write it down for me."

That same afternoon Poitier drove his truck down to somewhere more urban—Travis thought perhaps San Jose—and returned with a California driver's license and a Social Security number for his newest employee. Sure enough, the license listed his name as Skate McHenry and his age as eighteen. The address was the same as the motel's. When Travis looked surprised, the owner shrugged and mumbled, "You can do just about anything if you know the right people."

The other boy was a small, well-muscled Mexican teenager with wavy black hair and large, deep-set brown eyes. His name was Alejandro Morales. Since they were to share one of the rooms of the motel, the newly legitimized Skate hoped they could become friends. Alejandro really *was* eighteen, and looked it. When Skate made the same claim, Alejandro, unlike Mr. Poyteer, had laughed.

"*Seguro*," he'd said. "If you're eighteen, *muchacho*, I'm a hundred and two. If you're eighteen, I'm a hippopotamus. If you're…"

"Hey!" Skate had snapped. "I *need* to be eighteen, so I am. Okay?"

Alejandro grinned. "Okay," he said. "I always wanted to be a hippopotamus."

Work hours were long but not onerous. Her-*cool*, as he asked to be called, insisted the restaurant be swept out early in the morning, before the doors opened at 7 am and after they closed at 11 pm. In between, Skate polished the rails on the counter and cleaned the Naugahyde coverings of the banquettes and chairs. He washed the large picture windows inside and out and wiped down all the glass surfaces of the framed bromides that covered the walls—"In God We Trust, All Others Pay Cash," "I'm on the gin and tonic diet; so far I've lost 2 days," "Why exercise and punish my body for something my mouth did?" Skate's favorite became, "I can only please one person a day. Today isn't your day. Tomorrow doesn't look good either." There were dozens of others.

Skate washed dishes when there were dishes to wash and discovered he enjoyed it. It'd been boring to wash two plates, two spoons, two forks and two cups for his father, with a shallow sink and a barely trickling warm water faucet. Washing a quantity of dishes, however, with a deep basin, a huge, hard spray of hot water whooshing from a widely maneuverable hose—and with mountains of suds—was exciting. Fun. Like washing his car. He even enjoyed pulling on the yellow rubber gloves, imagining himself a Grand Prix driver just before he slipped behind the wheel.

He liked the sparkling white plates. No nicks, no scratches. Spotless! *Swishing and sloshing, swishing and sloshing*—was sloshing a word? A sing-song rhythm entered his head: *Swishing and sloshing, the plates become clean/ Prettiest plates that I've ever seen/swiping and wiping/will make the plates dry….* He thought a moment. *We do it with air/I can't tell you why.* Hah! That was fun. Silly, but fun.

As instructed by their boss, Skate and Alejandro together changed sheets, pillowcases and towels daily in the motel units when they were occupied. As he soon learned from Alejandro, that meant one or two families a week during the winter season and three or four during the spring and summer. Fall, for some reason, was the heaviest time of all. Skate and Alejandro together prepared the laundry for a twice-weekly pickup. Alejandro's individual responsibilities were to do the cooking when Hercule was engaged in keeping the books, ordering supplies, or away on errands. Alejandro also cleaned the kitchen, except for washing dishes, and repaired the pickup truck and any other motorized devices not found to be in tip-top working order.

Alejandro was an excellent mechanic, and he was fascinated by Skate's Essex. He spent as much time as he could examining the complexities of its engine, its suspension, its camshafts, its transmission, electrical system, cooling system, and all the rest. Like Hercule, he never asked how or why a somewhat less than eighteen-year old boy had come into possession of such a grand old car. To Skate's immeasurable relief.

It was during one of Alejandro's earliest examinations of the Essex that he came across what Skate kept stored under the back seat.

"Whoa!" he said. "*Amigo*! You're loaded for bear!"

"Naw, not really," Skate shrugged, wishing he'd controlled the exploration, trying to keep his anxiety contained. "Squirrels, rabbits, doves. Like that. Nothing too big. A varmint gun. Still, I'd appreciate it if you didn't tell anyone."

"No problem, *muchacho*." Alejandro made a gesture as if turning a key to lock his lips.

The two boys began swapping stories, mostly because Alejandro loved to talk. Such conversations usually took place as they lay in their separate beds just before midnight, ready to sleep after their long day. Skate was reluctant to confide much at first, and many of his stories were fictitious, though he strove to plant a kernel of truth in each. He assumed—having no reason to think otherwise—that most of Alejandro's stories were true.

The Mexican lad soon revealed that both his parents were dead.

Well, thought Skate. We have that in common.

In fact, Alejandro told him, his folks had perished in a nearby automobile accident. They were sightseeing not far from Ray's peak when a freak rainstorm swept the mountain, reduced the visibility to almost zero, and made the road super-slick. The car slithered off the road and toppled into a ravine, where it had tumbled end-over-end until both car and occupants lay in a mangled mess at the cliff's soggy bottom.

Skate learned that, unlike his own parents, Alejandro's had been well-educated. Had both gone to university in Mexico. In fact they'd met at the *Universidad de Guadalajara*, both students in the Fine Arts program, where Jorge studied poetry and Mariana painting. Only a few years after graduation, trying to support themselves, their infant son, and Jorge's widowed mother and finding it impossible to make a living in their chosen professions, they'd decided to join the migrant hordes in the US, working the summer harvest of cotton and grain from Yuma, Arizona up to and through California's Great Central Valley, sometimes even the fruit harvest that reached up further, into Oregon and Washington. The accident that took his parents' lives occurred toward the end of one grain-harvesting season, when they'd taken Alejandro away from the hot valley for a brief mountain vacation. On that occasion, they'd decided to stay at the same motel where both boys now worked. One morning they had spirited themselves away for an early tryst, just the two of them, leaving the sixteen-year old Alejandro to sleep. A day later, when the accident was discovered, Hercule was quick to pay the funeral costs, and offered the boy a job and a place to stay. That was two years ago; he'd been here ever since.

"What's Mr. Poitier—Her-*cool*—really like?" Skate asked Alejandro a few weeks after they'd begun working together. "Seems nice enough. Got me that ID and everything. Never yells. Pay's just okay but he seems like a pretty good boss. Am I right?"

An image of his father suddenly flashed through his mind. "But sometimes he seems glum. Doesn't he? Mopes about for no reason I can see."

Hands behind his head against a pillow, Alejandro shrugged one shoulder and thought a moment.

"Well, yeah," he said. "But people are complicated. You know? He's nice enough, I guess. Until he isn't."

"*Cómo?* What's that supposed to mean?"

Alejandro smiled, pleased and amused that Skate was trying to learn a little Spanish. It seemed like every time Alejandro used a Spanish word, Skate asked what it meant and tried to use it himself at the next opportunity. "Well," he said, "you've never seen him when he's drunk."

"I've never seen him even *take* a drink! Doesn't seem hung over in the mornings either."

Alejandro laughed. "Because he's on the wagon, *amigo*. But when he falls off—"

"You've seen this?"

"Have I ever! Listen, *muchacho*. If I've never seen Hercule Poitier absolutely shit-faced fuckin' drunk then I'm a—"

"Yeah, I know. You're a hippopotamus."

Alejandro chuckled. "He's what they call a binge drinker. To be fair, I've only seen it twice in the two years I've been here. Both times it was a woman. Some *puta* comes along and hooks up with him for awhile. Then one night they get stupid drunk and high on bennies and bingo! Shouting and glass-breaking time, man! Twice I've seen the police called. I believe he even kicked one of his *putas* in the stomach. But she didn't press charges, or his ass would've been in jail."

"Ummph. Yeah. People can do crazy things when they're drunk. My father used to whip me til I bled."

Alejandro shook his head in sympathy. They were quiet a moment. Then: "You know he's an ex-con, right?"

"What?! No shit! He's been in prison?"

"Twenty years, man. Alcatraz. Killed some guy in a knife fight. Told me so himself. Served his full sentence, then after he got out, opened this place. Been here ever since. I don't know who bankrolled him, but my guess is that's why he's able to get us those IDs and things, right? Knows a lot of gangsters back in Oakland. I saw someone up here one day, talking to him. *Un pinche cabrón*, man."

"Cómo?

"One scary-looking motherfucker."

Skate fell quiet. It took him less than a second to conjure up the image of a scary-looking motherfucker.

One evening Skate watched as Alejandro pulled out a dog-eared book from his nightstand, switched on his bed lamp, and began reading. Skate knew what the book was, the most favored of the several he kept in his drawer.

"So your dad was a poet?"

"One book of poetry. Just one. If he hadn't had to work so hard, he'd probably have done more. Or if he'd lived longer."

"What was he like, your dad?"

"Strict, but kind. Had principles. An interest in his fellow man. High ideals, y'know? And he loved to write. You into poetry?"

"Not sure. Haven't read much. Ma used to read me some. Like 'The Highwayman' and 'The Raven.' Those are the only ones I remember. And, oh, yeah, stuff by Edgar A. Guest. I mean, sometimes, just for fun, I invent little rhyming things. Every once in a while. You know, silly stuff I make up."

"Oh, yeah? Hey, that's good! I think my dad called that stuff doggerel verse. La poesía burlesca. Or *coplas de ciega*, something like that, if bad. Easy rhythms, easy rhymes. Usually intended to be funny. He wrote some too, he told me. Every poet does it, he said. And it can be clever or it can be terrible. But that wasn't his serious stuff. The stuff he was proudest of."

"Was he good, your father?"

Alejandro shrugged. "There's all levels, you know? I think my dad was pretty good and I enjoy his poetry, like what's in this book—his only one—but there are better poets in the Spanish language, as he'd have been the first to tell you. Now. Spanish poetry is great, man. I mean *great*. So my father's stuff is okay but my favorite lines are by Garcia Lorca. Listen to this: '*Las lágrimas amordazan al viento. Y no se oye otra cosa que el llanto.*'" He recited slowly, in a voice that surprised Travis with its drama.

"Sounds nice. Don't know what it means, but it sounds heavy. Am I right?"

Alejandro, looking at the window pane, or perhaps beyond, at the night sky, had fallen quiet.

"Like I said," continued Skate. "I like the way it sounds, but I wish I knew what it *meant*."

"Yeah, I heard. Well, translating is hard, *muchacho*. *Lágrimas* means tears, *llanto* means crying. *Viento* means wind. *Amordazar* means, like, to muzzle, like you muzzle a dog? Or to gag. So the first line is something like 'Tears gag the wind.'"

"*Gag*? That's…pretty ugly! Isn't it supposed to be beautiful?"

"Well, yes! Of course! And the Spanish is beautiful, *amigo*. believe me. But, see. That's the trouble. That's just what I can manage by way of translating. So…you have to say…something like that."

"Gag! *Yuk*!" After a minute, Skate said, "How about 'smother'? How about, 'Tears *smother* the wind'?"

Alejandro thought a moment.

"Hey, that's quite good, I think! 'Tears smother the wind!' How about that! Anyway, the second line is, "There can't be heard any other sound except the crying."

Skate looked away a moment.

"No sound can be heard but the crying," he said finally. "No, make that 'weeping.' 'No sound can be heard…'"

"'…but the weeping.' Cool! That's good, *amigo!* You got a gift, you know that?"

"Whatever. In any case, I love the sounds. I really do."

And he meant it. Something had stretched inside him. A fullness was visiting. A swelling. An excitement. Like when he'd spotted the condor on the mesa. "Maybe I *should* read some poetry. Some real poetry."

"*Si, cómo no?* Start with Dylan Thomas, maybe. A Welsh poet, but he writes in English. Like Lorca, he was in love with words. *Palabras son importante, amigo.* Words are important."

Maybe, Skate thought. But as he rolled over and prepared to douse his lamp, he wondered: If I'd had the right words, could I have stopped my father from beating me? Could the right words have saved me from becoming a killer?

His finger paused on the light switch as his mind was jarred suddenly into another thought: *Was that what he was now? A killer?*

Chapter 5

SOUTHEAST CITY, WASHINGTON, 1965

Maddie, Rusty

It was three weeks into their relationship before Maddie stayed over. The next day, as they lay there in the aftermath of having said good morning the only way they knew how, she asked, "Don't you want to know anything about me?"

He was quiet a moment. "Like what? Anything you want to tell?"

"I'm married."

He fiddled with the bedclothes a minute.

"And I have a son."

He closed his eyes. Almost imperceptibly, his breathing deepened. In his quietest possible voice, he said, "So where's your boy?"

This wasn't the question she expected. "With my mother in Yakima. He's seven."

"Husband?"

That was the question. She took a deep breath. "Part of that population the other side of Route 12."

He grunted and nodded.

Southeast City's two claims to prominence within the state were two institutions situated there: a small liberal arts college with a national reputation, and the main branch of the state prison system.

"What's he in for?"

"Petty theft and kiting checks, that's how it began. But he graduated later to holding up filling stations and convenience stores. Last time with a gun. I mean, this is his second time caught. Served eighteen months a while back, then wound up in prison again."

"How long this time?"

"Five years. Served three so far."

He didn't tell her he'd been sure she had a relative in the hoosegow from the beginning, since she lived in a trailer a few blocks from the lockup. Their first time together had been in that trailer, when she'd invited him in wearing his gift of nylons and very little else, while a phonograph played The Drifters' "Nylon Stockings and Golden Earrings."

"Uh huh. So. You still love him?"

She answered quickly, as if she'd rehearsed it, or at least thought about it a lot. "Did I ever? is what I ask. At one time, I guess. I must have, right? We met young and silly, in high school. Then he lights out and I don't see him for another bunch of years. A decade almost. Then comes back into town and starts puttin' the moves on me. He'd been around by then, done some bad things I never got told about. Oh, he was smooth, all right. And before I developed some sense, I was pregnant. Since he's been in prison, I've filed for divorce twice—but he won't sign the papers."

"Does he need to?"

"So my lawyer says."

He tossed back the covers, swung his knees over the side of the bed. "Sounds like you need to get you a new lawyer. That is, if you really wanna get shed of him."

"Don't be doubtin' me now, Rusty. I'm doin' the best I can."

"I know. I'll fix us some breakfast. Pancakes okay?"

"Fine." She sat there a moment longer, propped up against the pillow, staring into space. "How come you never tell me anything about yourself?"

He busied himself with his kitchen implements, took down a box of Bisquick from a cupboard shelf, found milk and an egg in the refrigerator, all before answering. "What's to tell?" he tried. "I am what you see. An open book."

She snorted and began to dress. "Closed book, more like it. Closed and with a chain around it. I see what you are now, but I don't know where you've been, what you've done. You had some history before Southeast City, I'm sure. For all I know you could be a serial killer."

His lips tightened. A slight frown crossed his face but he was careful to turn away so she wouldn't see. He answered, "Shredded wheat or Post Toasties?"

It took her a minute to hear his pun. Then she laughed. "Okay, smart ass," she said. "Still, just another evasion, Mr. Deep Mystery."

One pancake was already bubbling on the griddle before he spoke again. "Give it time, Maddie. "

"That one."

He observed the kittens. Five in the cage they were crouched in front of. The one she'd suggested was the friskiest, a furry dynamo black as anthracite, that kept plunging headlong into the others, attacking their hindquarters with a faux-ferocious nip or rearing up on its tiny back legs in mock fear and surprise. Sometimes, as a result of the latter move, it tumbled over backwards.

A slight smile on his face, Rusty seemed lost in thought, while Maddie fell silent, shifting her weight from one haunch to another. The girl who had brought them to the cage, a scrawny teenager chewing gum and sighing periodically, looked on with folded arms.

"Done," he said finally.

It had been Maddie's suggestion that he seek another cat. In fact, she'd pestered him about it. So they had driven out to the animal shelter on Melrose and North Wilbur on a Saturday to look over the prospects. She'd taken the afternoon off, and so had he.

"I perceive," she said, "that—like me—you're not superstitious."

"You perceive, do you? Well, you perceive right."

"Whatcha gonna name him, then?"

"You so sure it's a him?"

"It is," said the young caretaker, and cracked her gum. He rubbed his chin.

"*Schorl*," he said.

"Schorl! What on earth is that?"

"A mineral. From the tourmaline family."

"Oh, well that explains everything. Rusty, I swear you know the strangest things. Why Schorl?"

"Just came to me. It's black, of course."

"Oh, of course! So. You want to tell me how you know this?"

He stood, dusting the knees of his pants. "Some things just stay with you, I guess."

After they ferried the kitten back to his bungalow, he put out a saucer of milk that the cat attacked hungrily. A good deal of milk wound up on Schorl's whiskers or the floor, while they looked on and laughed. Later, Rusty unbent a coat hanger from his closet, attached a rag to one end. Their amusement continued for the better part of twenty minutes, each taking turns to see who could provoke the cat into higher leaps. Afterwards, he arranged an old pile of underwear in a corner of the kitchen and the kitten curled up and went to sleep. They stood watching him a while, then she turned and looked at him. She pouted.

"You're an interesting man, Rusty Thomas. I don't know what to make of you."

He took her in his arms. "Don't make more of me than I am, Maddie. Really. As it turns out, I think quite highly of *you*."

They kissed, and soon it was she who urged him toward the bedroom. "While the cat sleeps," she said.

"Where were you born? Where'd you grow up? Who were your mama and papa?"

As her questions tumbled out, he cupped the pillow around his ears, then released it.

"Oh, my. We've come this far. Why ask now, when you didn't then?"

"Wasn't important then. Is now."

"Why now?"

She rolled over close and poked him sharply in the ribs several times, until he laughed and gathered her to him. Then she crawled on top of him and lay there, her cheek against his neck, her small body sprawled out across his long slender one like a piece of seaweed on a slab of rock.

Chapter 6

ARIZONA, WASHINGTON, OREGON, 1952-59

Skate/Robert, Alejandro

Two years passed. Sometimes it almost seemed to Skate that he'd always done this work, that Alejandro had always been his buddy. Both boys grew older, of course, but the physical change in Skate was marked. He had a spurt the summer he turned sixteen and was a six-footer by that fall. By his second year at the Skyline Motel-Lodge he looked eighteen even though he was only seventeen and his driver's license claimed he was twenty. Alejandro barely appeared to change.

In their comings and goings at the motel, and at the restaurant as well, they could hardly avoid observing customers, including families, and sometimes, in particular, girls or young women whom each of them found attractive.

They would sometimes discuss the tugs and pulls of their observations and their yearnings in the evening, before going to sleep. In such shared moments they might laugh or sigh. But whatever fantasies each might entertain, in the real world neither crossed the line even into casual conversation. They confined themselves to an occasional nod or the odd smile. Longings were kept on a tight leash. Each was aware, not only of how inappropriate mingling with customers might look—they were the *help* after all—but how much their jobs depended on strict reticence and resolve. Circumspect to the point of primness in their behavior, each kept his secrets locked up tight, except with each other.

Their roles at the restaurant became less differentiated. Alejandro sometimes washed dishes; Skate often cooked. Alejandro sometimes went on errands to San Jose or elsewhere, at Hercule's orders, and in the company truck, though he never felt comfortable doing so, fearing that his own questionable immigration status might be discovered.

By and large, Hercule remained a decent, accommodating employer, depressed on occasion, but not in a way that affected his two employees adversely, except that such moments led to a little more work on their part, which they rarely minded. By the end of the second year they'd received two raises—to eighty-five and then to ninety-five cents an hour—and were often praised by their boss. Without warning then, in late spring, two years almost to the day since Travis Mackey became Skate McHenry, a calamitous din arose in the middle of the night. Both boys shuddered awake to the sound of hoarse shouting and breaking glass.

They had long prepared for this. Had been, in fact, on particularly high alert since the arrival three days before of a perhaps once-pretty but now ravaged, coarse-looking peroxide blonde named Marla. So, proceeding according to plan from the moment the fracas began, they rose silently, slipped on their jeans and pullovers, packed their few belongings, and carried them to the Essex, whose tank was kept full. Within fifteen minutes of the first thrown vase or shattered mirror, they were on the back roads leading out of town. Each was owed a paycheck, but that was a small concern under the circumstances, both having squirreled away most of their salaries in preparation for an hour they knew would come. Not risking involvement with the law was an important goal for each of them.

Within an hour of leaving the Skyline Motel and Lodge along back roads, they were skirting San Jose. In another hour they were hurtling down the long, flat ribbon of Highway 99 in the heart of the San Joaquin Valley, headed for Arizona.

On the trip to Yuma, which took three-and-one-half days because they were careful with the Essex, they were stopped in the desert by a snapped fan belt and, again, by a flat tire. While the ever resourceful Alejandro was fixing each of these mishaps, Skate took out his Savage Model 24—the .22/410—and bagged a jackrabbit with the shotgun. Since it was nearing nightfall anyway, and they were hungry, they pulled off the road and found enough dead mesquite branches to start a fire, enabling them to roast the rabbit. Skate cleaned; Alejandro cooked. They agreed it was a fabulous meal, though Alejandro did complain he almost broke a tooth on an undiscovered shotgun pellet.

On the road again, still licking his chops at the memory of their satisfying meal, Skate said, "You realize I'm going to want to change my name again, right?"

Alejandro was quiet.

"It's too important that what I did not be discovered. I don't want to risk it."

They'd become like brothers. Alejandro, by this time, knew all the salient points of Skate's past, and vice versa. A trust had grown between them, a closeness of a kind that Skate had not felt since his mother died and that Alejandro had missed since losing his parents.

"Okay, *muchacho*," he said finally. "I understand. I have an uncle in Yuma who can help with that. If he's not been sent back already himself."

At dawn the next day they arrived in the near-border town of Yuma and were greeted like long lost children by Alejandro's remaining relatives.

So Alejandro and his newly named friend, Robert Porter, worked together for the better part of two more years, picking cotton, harvesting grain, picking fruit. They would travel up from Arizona through the entire length of California and on up further through Oregon into Washington. Robert was indifferent to fruit-picking, though he loved the smells while he was doing it. But he absolutely hated cotton-picking, was never good at it. For someone as tall as he, it was back-breaking work. He never seemed to master the double-fisted technique that the shorter, squatter Alejandro so ably employed, striding down the center of the row, plucking with both hands at once. Whenever they'd come to the weigh-in, Alejandro would have more than doubled Robert's output and they were paid by the pound.

Working the grain harvest, on the other hand, though hard and dirty labor, was more enjoyable to Robert, chiefly because it involved driving. During the first year both he and Alejandro drove grain trucks, each carrying several tons of grain—wheat, barley or flax—to be weighed, recorded and deposited in the local silos. Much time was spent waiting at the side of the field for the combines to reach the near edge, where they would empty their bins into the back of the young men's trucks, but they used that interval for reading, a habit Robert had picked up from Alejandro. Alejandro somehow knew where the libraries were in every small town along the route, and they would surrender the books they had borrowed at the end of their one-or two-week stint in the area.

Robert's second year of harvest offered him less time to read but was more exciting and lucrative since, at his pleading—hounding, really—the crew boss finally relented and tried him out jockeying a combine. It was a challenging yet satisfying job, especially when the turf was uneven, since the rotating blades had to be continually raised and lowered by inches in order to thrash grain but not scrape dirt, while at the same time assuring that the enormous, unwieldy machine moved steadily toward the opposing ditch bank along the prescribed path; it required unwavering attention, and Robert proved adept at it. The downside was that, after twelve or thirteen hours of this you were caked with dirt and chaff, you were thoroughly exhausted, and you were left with no time to read.

It was early morning. Alejandro had just finished tuning up the Essex when Robert asked, "How much more time you think we have on this old buggy, Alejandro? How many years?"

They were staying at an apple orchard just outside of Renton, in northwest Washington. It was nearly two years since they'd started harvesting together. The picking season had just ended, a day earlier than expected. Many of the workers had already left. A few still slept in the bunkhouse.

"So long as I'm around, I can probably keep it going for

a couple more, Roberto. But it's gonna start gettin' mighty difficult to find parts to fit this old girl. They might have to be machine-tooled special. I think you should be looking around to try to sell, *muchacho*. There are bound to be collectors out there for a fine old machine like this. Check the newspapers. With the money you get you could buy you a serviceable used pickup and still have lots of money left over for a rainy day."

Robert smiled, then looked concerned. He stretched his hand out, casting a glance at the rising sun, just a few inches up over the Pacific. "Expecting rain?" he asked. Then he froze.

A cloud of dust was streaking in their direction, bearing down fast. Two panel trucks, approaching at breakneck speed.

"Holy shit!" said Alejandro. "Robert, roust the guys in the bunk house! Aw, shit! *Roto cabrón*! It's too late."

They were already in the yard, a swarm of them, tumbling out of their trucks, cuffs dangling. Several sprinted for the bunkhouse. They took one look at Robert, made him for a gringo and passed on by, clamping Alejandro in handcuffs immediately. Out of the corner of his eye Robert saw that one picker from their crew, Antonio, had fled through a bunkhouse side door and was sprinting through the orchard, only to be tackled and taken into custody.

Robert watched in helpless silence as the men were loaded into the panel trucks to be taken away. Just before the doors closed he saw Alejandro bring his fingers to his lips and twist them like a key turning a lock. Even without that gesture, Robert would have been certain his secrets were safe. But he vowed at that moment never to share the burden of his past with anyone again.

He entered the bunk house. Bedclothes and possessions in disarray. He lingered over Alejandro's tidy bunk, which his friend had made up promptly upon rising this morning, just as he had always done seemingly so long ago at the Skyline Motel Lodge in Sequoiaville.

Staring at Alejandro's bed, Robert made a decision. No more grain harvest. No more Yuma. No more San Joaquin Valley. It was back to the high country now. Back to the condors. He would search for a life in the mountains. He would become a logger.

As he turned to go, something caught his eye, the corner of a book peeping out from under the pillow. It was the book of poems by Alejandro's father. He rummaged further. In the nightstand he found Alejandro's Lorca, containing the poem whose famous line he'd first recited to him. He would take both volumes, knowing his friend would have wished this. They were Alejandro's parting gifts.

He started to open the Lorca, then stopped, because he realized he knew by heart the lines he was seeking: *"Las lágrimas amordazan al viento / y no se oye otra cosa que el llanto.* Tears smother the wind / And no sound can be heard but the weeping."

Chapter 7
SOUTHEAST CITY, WASHINGTON, 1965
Maddie, Rusty, Sammy

Cap off, head in his hands, Rusty sat on a carton in the shipping room. Would it ever stop? He kept hoping to change things, make them normal again, whatever that meant. But once you start running, he wondered, can you ever stop? He ached sometimes to let his guard down, come clean, trust someone. He ached to learn more about poetry. To study birds seriously. To love.

Suddenly, he grabbed his cap and clipboard and rushed back through the cooking room toward his appointed tasks.

"Why do you keep that shotgun in the corner of your kitchen?"

They were on their way to Yakima in Rusty's pickup. The job at the pea-canning factory had ended and he'd decided to take a few days off before looking for other work. It had been his idea to visit her son.

Not just a shotgun, he wanted to say. Shotgun and rifle combo. But why do that? Assuming an innocent expression, he said, "Where would you like me to keep it?"

"No, silly! I mean, you don't hunt or anything. Why have it around at all?"

"Just inherited it. A family thing, I guess. I could hunt if I wanted to. I have done so. I'll put it in the closet if you like. Or under the bed?"

She sighed and fidgeted, looked out the window again. They were beginning to climb once more. A dozen miles more and they would drop down into Yakima and find her mother's place.

"You don't tell me much, Rusty Thomas. I'm not even sure that's your real name."

He could feel the blood beating behind his ear.

"I know, Maddie. And I'm sorry for it. I will tell you one day. I will, I promise." Then he added, "But when I do…you'll need to keep it secret, hear?"

They pulled up in front of a modest pitched-roof white house on South Sixteenth Street, a few blocks east of the railroad tracks. A small porch was edged by a faux-Georgian wrought-iron handrail. A cracked concrete walkway divided a lawn that was all scattered clumps of grass. A garden hose curled around from the side of the house toward a red plastic wading pool, and beside the pool, stood a boy in yellow bathing trunks. A towhead. Though the sun beat down hard, he was clutching a towel and shivering. Small for his age, Rusty thought. The moment Maddie opened the door, he ran higgledy-piggledy across the lawn and leaped into her arms.

She staggered back against the car, laughing, hugging him.

"Whoa, little guy! Though not so little any more, hey? Heavy as a rock, you."

A figure appeared behind the house's screen door as Rusty circled round the car.

"Sammy, say hello to Mr. Thomas. Mama, come on out, why don'tcha?"

Rusty and Sammy shook hands as Mrs. Thornton moved slowly across the lawn, smiling, limping slightly, drying her hands on her apron.

"Hello, daughter," she said, enfolding Maddie in her arms. "Pleased to meet you, Mr. Thomas."

"Likewise, ma'am. Sammy, you're much bigger than I expected. You sure you're only seven? I would have guessed twenty-one, maybe twenty-two."

The boy giggled, ducked behind his mother. "I don't think so," he said in a restrained voice.

The afternoon unfolded quietly enough, sometimes in conversation, sometimes not, though Rusty and Sammy did go outdoors at one point to toss around a baseball Rusty had brought as a present, along with a pair of fielder's mitts. Rusty found the boy, though shy and subdued at first, eventually quite friendly. Later, the four of them dined on baked chicken with cornbread stuffing and heaps of steaming green beans and carrots, served in the back yard. Rusty decided that Sammy reminded him of himself at that age, when his mother was still alive. He made a mental note to tell Maddie that later, but then wondered whether it might open a door he didn't want to walk through. Mrs. Thornton—Peggy—he found quite pleasant, though wary at first. She struck him as someone who'd been beaten down over time. Or had she always been that way? He felt grateful she showed no eagerness to pry into her daughter's choice of boyfriend. But by the end of the afternoon he'd developed a sense that she approved. Her husband—Maddie's father—had died before his grandson was born, she told him. Photographs on the mantelpiece revealed a small, good-looking, bald man in khakis and suspenders, proudly displaying his bowling trophies.

After dinner they watched television until Sammy's bedtime, and then—Rusty was surprised but gratified by Maddie's suggestion—he read the boy a story from a pile of books beside his bed. After Sammy had nodded off, Maddie tucked him in. They watched him sleeping for a few minutes, their arms around each other, hugging fiercely after they were sure he was a goner, then kissing and touching each other until they came to their senses. It was eleven o'clock before they began the three-hour drive back to Southeast City.

"Great kid, Maddie," Rusty said as they sought the highway.

"You got that right," she said. "Wish I could be with him more. I send a little money every month. What I can. He's a burden on mama, of course, but he's so much better off—better treated—than when Vinnie was around. Vinnie used to whup him something awful."

"Really?"

A moment of fraught silence, of spectral darkness. Rusty recalled the feel of his father's razor strop against his legs and buttocks—the rawness, the blood—then repeated his question, with a tone less charged.

"Oh, yeah. Cuffed me around a bit too," she said.

"That scar on your forehead?"

"Yep. Had to call the cops on him coupla times."

This was the last they spoke before Maddie, resting her head against the window, fell asleep.

Chapter 8
MONTANA, 1970/71
Clayton, Jake, Marjorie

This morning the cold felt bracing. Other times he might have shivered, pounded his arms around his torso, flexed his fingers repeatedly inside his gloves. Complained even. Not that, save the odd stranger, there was anyone to complain to.

Ahead of him was not a familiar, well-marked trail. But he didn't mind that. Rather liked striking out on his own, across the mountain, knowing that a town, a town new to him, lay on the other side, nestled in a pleasant, stream-fed valley. So the map said, and Clayton Poole believed in maps, loved reading them, loved following them, loved the way one could take a rugged, up-and-down wandering-all-over-the-place reality and transform it into a flat graphic grid from which one could take clear and proper guidance to find one's way.

He moved forward at a reasonable pace all day, pausing only for ten minutes or so in mid-afternoon to watch in thrall as a pair Golden Eagles locked talons in the fall sky and swung each other around like square dancers— their courtship ritual. They were the first examples of the *Aquila genus* he'd seen on his three-day trek across the Bitterroots, and he felt excited— privileged even—to watch them mating. Very few people had witnessed this. This was beautiful country all right. This was the way it was supposed to be.

In early evening he stopped to eat. He'd opened a can of beans from his knapsack and was consuming it hungrily when something stopped him. An instinct, perhaps, or had he heard something? Yes, there it was. The call came faintly, so spare and frail that he at first had difficulty winnowing it from the chatter of birds acknowledging the arrival of twilight. He'd already recognized the *ki ki ki* of the Northern Flicker and the vibrating two-note *tom-tom* of the Great Horned Owl. But was there something more? He lowered the container of beans to the leafy ground cover, licked his lower lip and held still. There it was, pale but certain. A woman's voice. Calling for help.

He stood, swiveled his head this way and that, trying to fix the direction. When he thought he had it, he began to walk, picking his way carefully among the trees and brambles, moving quietly to stay in contact with the sound. In addition to the word *Help!* he heard a gentle moan, and then a caught breath, almost a sob. It grew stronger, and a moment later he spotted her. She lay among a waffle of leaves, moaning and rolling her head.

She had dark hair and brows and wore a long dress, which was torn and caught at the bottom, he could see, for her leg was held tight in the teeth of a metal trap. The leg looked both bloody and swollen, its flesh gashed and the ankle likely broken. But why had she gone out in her house slippers?

"Stay still!" he commanded. "Here. Let me free you."

The trap was strong. Probably the target had been a wolf or a bobcat, but it had certainly made a mess of her leg. "Can you gently pull your leg out if I pry it apart?" he asked. He managed to wrestle it open and she dragged her useless limb out of it, shrieking in pain. "Sorry," he said. "There. You're free. Now, where is the nearest house? Where do you need to go?"

She lifted her arm feebly and pointed. Down the mountain. Good. He squatted, shoveled her into his arms. She had length to her but was surprisingly light, as if the long bones were filled with air. When he struggled to his feet he stood a moment, taking in a few markers, so he could return later for his bedroll, utensils and journals.

The place she'd pointed to was farther than expected. She fainted and revived several times. He kept praying they were going the right way. The leaf cover was fierce, with uncertain footing beneath, dropped branches, twigs, gullies. To keep his mind away from feeling the effort of managing her weight, he recited poems he knew. First Auden, and then a Spanish poem, the only one he knew by heart. At last, on the cusp of his own strength failing, he spotted the house. *A* house. He hoped it was the right one, but it no longer mattered. He could go no further. He made it to the door before collapsing on the porch, calling out. A moment later a man flung open the door and together they managed to carry her into the house.

The light came so hard and sharp through the window that the moment it fell on his face he stirred and awoke. He was in a bed of goose down, with a comforter over the top of him; it was a moment before he remembered where and why. It had been awhile since he'd slept in a bed of any kind. A knock came lightly on the door. Not too lightly: a man's rap.

The door opened slightly and a face appeared, rugged features and a mane of ashen hair. "Mornin'."

"Morning," replied Clayton. He struggled to remember the man's name.

"They's breakfast on the table. Already a bit late but didn't want to wake you. Seemed like you needed sleep."

"Thanks. I appreciate it. Thanks for putting me up."

"Least I could do. Mr. Poole, is it?"

"That's right," grinned Clayton. "And you're… Henderson, I believe?"

"Call me Jake." He hesitated a moment. "The missus is resting. She slept pretty peaceful, considering. 'Course Doc gave her a shot of morphine would've stopped a cow."

Clayton nodded. "Glad she's doing okay. I'll get up now."

He lay there another minute or two after Jake closed the door, feeling the late autumn light from the window, remembering the woman he'd carried down the mountain, how light she'd been, how far they'd gone.

Which reminded him: As soon as he'd had breakfast, he would recover his belongings. Since he'd left an open, half-filled can of beans beside his back-pack, he could only hope everything hadn't been destroyed by the local wildlife.

An hour or so later, after returning from the trail with his possessions, Clayton visited the farmer in the barn, where he was mucking out the horse stall. Jake leaned his arms on his shovel a moment and asked whether his guest would like to stick around for awhile. He could bunk for free, Jake said, all he'd need to do is a few chores each day.

"I've got the space since my daughters are growed and away from here. I wouldn't ask much. You can stay for a little or for longer. I owe you, Mr. Poole. And the missus could prob'ly use the company as well. While she recovers."

Clayton rubbed his chin, leaned back against the timber of the barn door.

"That's nice of you," he said finally. "Tell you what. I'd like to go into town this afternoon, see what it's like. It's sorta where I was headed, though I've never been here before, only spotted it on a map. Let me walk into town and check it out and I'll be back later on tonight. That sound all right?"

"That'd be fine. Don't wanna pressure you none. It's just here, is all. And I'm beholden to you, Mr. Poole. I surely am."

"Sounds like it might work out. At least for awhile. Until I get my bearings and decide what I want to do."

"That's all I'm saying."

"Good. Okay. See you later then."

As Clayton turned away, Henderson called out, "Take the pickup if you like. Keys are behind the visor."

"Thanks, but that's okay. I'm used to walking."

Snow began early that year, but the snow treads on the Henderson pickup were up to the task. Only twice was the snow so bad that they were holed up in the farmhouse waiting for plows to clear the road into town. And Jake kept a pair of snowshoes on the back porch that Clayton used on occasion.

Evenings after dinner the two men, Clayton and Jake, sat in front of the fire that Jake had laid in the living room fireplace while Marjorie dozed or slept in the bedroom he and his wife had once shared. Jake had taken to sleeping in the third bedroom, "so as not to disturb the missus." There was no television anywhere in the house. "We don't get good reception out here anyway." But Marjorie had a radio to keep her company if she needed it.

Jake would most times spend ten or fifteen minutes in the bedroom keeping company with his wife, before joining Clayton. Clayton wondered what the two talked about but never asked. Then Jake would lay the fire and they'd watch the cordwood become embers while warmth and shadows flickered. Early on Clayton would ask politely after Marjorie's condition and mood and Jake would reply either, "She's doin' fine" or "Seems to be okay." Just those two phrases, nothing more.

Sometimes Jake might offer a glass of cider or something stronger and, to be friendly, Clayton might accept, though he'd never developed much of a taste for liquor. Then a quiet conversation would usually ensue, about the town, or the weeks' events as reported in *The Rolling Hills Reporter*, a paper which was gathering a small reputation throughout the region. In April, President Nixon had ordered the invasion of Cambodia, escalating the Vietnam War, which had sparked protests around the country. Clayton discovered that Jake was sympathetic to the protesters and against the war, as he was, although he thought it best to steer clear of politics, and that seemed to happen by mutual agreement.

Work on the farm was a more frequent topic, especially after Jake began paying Clayton a small wage in addition to room and board. They'd talk about what had been done as well as what was to come. When soybeans were planted, when potatoes, when corn. And cows. Clayton sometimes commented on the idiosyncrasies of the two Jerseys he'd begun milking. "Amazing how distinct their personalities are," he said. "Bess is so placid, while Virginia you have to butt with your head every once in a while so she knows who's boss."

"You got that right," Jake responded. "Just like dogs. Or children. I'll bet you could find such traits in mice, if you just knew enough."

And when no obvious topic presented itself, the conversation floated along on quiet platitudes. "Always something," Jake might say, referring to the farm. "Sowing in spring, reaping in summer, you prob'ly know the drill. Winter we do repairs—plenty to mend—and try to make sure the animals stay alive. Hardly any down time at all."

Clayton would take a little pull on his beverage and nod. He confided nothing of his poetry, or his past.

For many weeks, as Clayton stayed on, his early afternoons were taken up in service as caretaker and companion to Marjorie, while Jake was out or away, attending to the major demands of the farm. It was clear from the first that she regarded Clayton as some kind of angel—Gabriel perhaps?—who had swooped down on his mighty wings to save her in her hour of trial. This embarrassed him, but Jake had asked him to keep her company, so he did.

And two weeks into their afternoon *tête-à-têtes* she'd swerved abruptly into a more personal mode.

"This marriage was more or less what you'd call a marriage of convenience, you know," she said, glancing away at the window, picking at her nails above the patchwork coverlet. Immediately, Clayton felt wary, fearful that knowing too many private details might set him at odds with Jake. But she needed to talk, so he listened. He found himself watching her closely as she spoke, the lovely, wide mouth compressed and tight, the deep-set brown eyes either wide open or shut in a firm line, as if in pain. How old was she? he wondered. His age? A trifle more? Clayton would be thirty-four come summer. He marked the struggle in her knotted forehead—a battle between reluctance and a need to unburden—and realized, to his surprise—he minded her revelations less than he'd expected. Did hearing of another's pain serve as anodyne to his own? Buffering memories he preferred to keep locked away?

Her name before her marriage to Henderson had been Congreve, she told him, and before that, Hawkins. From Texas, but raised by an aunt here in Montana, after her family perished in a tornado. She'd been four at the time. Survived by crawling into a bathtub, the only item not sucked up in the storm's maw. The flooring having been snatched right out from underneath it, the tub had been discovered in the middle of what had become bare ground, swept clean by the storm. Nary a pipe, nail nor patch of grass to be seen anywhere. Or such was the story her aunt gave.

Anyway, she told Clayton, when Jake Henderson emerged on the scene as a widower she was already a widow, having lost her hulking "grease monkey" of a husband—a beloved, adventuring brute of a man, as she described him—to a motorcycle accident.

"Damned skinny-tired Honda!" she huffed. "Told him he shoulda bought a Harley, but you think he'd listen? Anyways…."

As she faltered and drifted off, Clayton chose the moment to withdraw. He rose and stuffed his hat on his head. "Sounds like quite a guy. But I must be off now, Marjorie. Need to run into town now if I'm to get back in time to milk the cows. See you tomorrow."

He did see her the next day, of course, since it seemed to be expected and she was confined to her bed, still forbidden by her doctor to walk. Clayton realized that, aside from the few minutes Jake spent with her in the early evening, his was the only company she had. It was a particularly chilly afternoon, so she asked if he minded making tea for the two of them. He of course complied but once they were seated, she served up a plate of details that startled him with their intimacy. "So there I was!" she said. "A widow with few options. With 'robust and healthy appetites,' if you know what I mean."

Clayton kept his features immobile, though he felt blood rushing to his face. He hoped the pale winter light from the window was weak enough to disguise it. But perhaps she was too intent on her story to care.

"Oh, yeah!" she continued, with renewed vigor, but as if she were talking to herself, to the wall, or perhaps to the grease monkey she'd loved so well. Shockingly personal, at any rate. "My urges were close to getting the best of me!"

He saw her legs move under the quilt, the tubular bump of her cast stationary while the other leg meandered away. He looked down at the floor, clearing his throat softly. His mind momentarily left the room; drifted to a memory of Maddie, her lovely face against the door of his pickup, catching a few winks as they drove north toward Yakima to see her son, when moments earlier she'd been pestering him with questions about his past. *His* past. No, Marjorie, he told himself, there we don't go. He felt suddenly tense—panicked, almost—and struggled to tune back in to her narrative. Your job is to listen, he told himself.

Now she was busy explaining that when Jake, this farmer she'd barely heard of—whose own wife had died a few years earlier—came sashaying down the mountain and into town with his proposition, it seemed to make sense to her.

"What did I know?" she said, her whole body drooping. "Options were limited for the both of us."

In different ways, Clayton imagined. Her limitation, aside from how much she might require an outlet for her "urges," would be lack of money: how to provide for a more secure future? Where else was she going to find a widowed property owner with 300 acres of potatoes, turnips, safflower and alfalfa, plus a couple of cows, to his name? One who was already past the pandemonium of raising children?

His limitations, on the other hand, would likely involve a dearth of attractive women of a certain age—those who wouldn't be clamoring for babies—plus finding one who'd be willing to abide by the rigors of a country life-style. Only if each seeker were willing to forage farther afield, he supposed—say Missoula or beyond—could either have located a more suitable companion.

At any event, Marjorie was saying, she'd been waitressing at the local café, still nursing a broken heart, when Henderson walked in with his proposal.

"Felt a lot like a business deal," she said—the next day—when she picked up the story, remarkably enough, just where it had been dropped the day before.

"We just knew each other to nod and say hello. He asked Martin Randall, my boss, if I could take off a few minutes, then sat me down at a booth along the side wall. I was flattered that this well-off rancher—we called them ranchers even when there weren't any cattle—was taking an interest in me. He ordered food—whatever I wanted—and began to lay out his proposition."

She sighed then, looking down at her fingers, as if noticing them for the first time. She spread them out and made a clucking sound while she squirmed a bit under the quilt. "Could you pass me my fingernail polish, please? In that little drawer there? Thanks, Clayton."

She grew silent then, painting her nails. Still curious about the story, he soon found himself engrossed by her activity, watching her, stroke after stroke. Such concentration! Her brow furrowed and a wedge of tongue poked out, resting against the edge of her top lip. Stroke, stroke. It aroused him, which he found surprising. Unfurled him a bit.

One hand done, she switched to the other, then picked up her tale as if it had never been interrupted. Clayton tried to re-focus.

"Told me he was a man who'd never mistreat me. And hasn't. I certainly can't complain about that." But he'd told her during these negotiations, she said, as she'd continued to eat her syrup-sticky meal of flapjacks & sausage—half wondering whether the man had lost his marbles—that he did have his "expectations." Chief among these, he'd told her, were 'a clean house and three hot meals a day.'

His farmhouse had three bedrooms but they must agree—he stressed this—that, barring the intervention of serious illness, they would sleep together every night and he would expect conjugal relations once a week, *'rain, shine, or a bridge washed out.'* She looked off in the distance and snorted, remembering that moment.

Clayton smiled; there was in fact a bridge a short distance away, down the road that led into Rolling Hills. That was the route he'd walk most days, snow or no snow, after his visit with her, to buy the personal stuff he needed, or just to look around. Sometimes he'd also buy whatever the Henderson household required, from a list either Jake or Marjorie wrote out for him, although in those instances he drove the family pickup.

But here was the thing: although he often felt on edge during his visits with Marjorie, the hours spent with Jake were quite relaxing. Clayton became fond of the rancher. It helped that Jake didn't pry into Clayton's past, of course. But he sensed a moral depth in the man, who was generous with time, generous with money, and quick to express gratitude for anything Clayton did, whether around the farm or in the house. Jake seemed so straightforward that Clayton couldn't even imagine him as devious or cunning.

At the same time, it struck him as curious that the man had so little to say about his wife during the evenings they spent by the fire. Clayton could remember only two occasions. Once: "She's a fine, big-hearted woman, Marjorie is. But we've only been together about a year."

The other was a variant of the first, after which he added, "My first wife and I were together thirty-odd years."

Clayton tried to imagine what that might have been like. Almost as long as he'd walked the earth. What would it be like to be with a woman that long? There was only one woman he could imagine that happening with. And that memory he kept trying to put behind him for good. Would there come a time when it would get easier?

In their evenings together, Jake always sat straight as a pine tree in his easy chair. That posture reminded Clayton of his father. Fortunately, nothing else did. His father he remembered most as a brooder and a punisher, especially when he drank. Jake didn't seem that way at all. The older man's hands, whether offering a drink or turning the pages of the newspaper, were strong, callused; clearly he'd done farm work from the time he was a boy, and did yet. But they were kind hands. Clayton could never imagine them raised to beat a child with a razor strop.

The chores Clayton had agreed to perform in return for his room and board (and "some spending money," as Jake called it) were commonplace enough: milking the two Jerseys, mucking out the barn and grooming Old Faithful, the big gray gelding that was the only horse on the farm. Clayton suspected he'd been a draft horse at one time; a yoke and harness hung in the barn and an old plow leaned against the wall underneath it, but that had given way to the Farmall tractor also stationed there. Another task

Clayton performed was gathering eggs from the dozen or so Rhode Island Reds. Still another, feeding the hogs—two boars he suspected would be slaughtered come spring.

All this he did in the early morning, though of course he'd milk the Jerseys a second time come sundown. The collected milk—what wasn't scheduled for their own household—he'd pour into aluminum canisters he'd haul into town for use by a restaurant. Apparently the café, cheerfully labeled *MorningNoon&Night*—the same one, he supposed, where Marjorie had been wooed, if you could call it that—settled up with the farmer on a monthly basis. Some of those chores, the less physically demanding ones, Clayton guessed that Marjorie had been doing before her accident. Sometimes Clayton also helped out in the kitchen—his own idea—since he was no stranger to butcher knife and cutting board.

One evening, studying Jake's strong profile in the firelight—the hawkish nose and the square jaw—he began to wonder, how would this farmer be as a husband? He had no idea how accurate Marjorie's view of things was. Maybe it wasn't mostly 'what happened or didn't happen in the sack,' as she'd once implied. Clayton imagined that Jake might be hard to live with day-to-day. Especially for a woman like Marjorie, who struck him as particularly headstrong. Two stubborn people with very different attitudes toward the marriage.

He was pretty sure this Montana farmer liked things

done a certain way, the way he'd always known them to be done. On the other hand, he'd accommodated Clayton easily enough—a man he knew little about except what there was to surmise from his acts and his bearing. How much did Jake know now, he wondered, about the turn Marjorie's mind was taking? She still slept in a separate room from him; were those few minutes with her in the evening the only time they talked? Had physical intimacy fled the marriage altogether? And, if Jake didn't know how she felt by now, what would happen when he found out?

Chapter 9

SOUTHEAST CITY, WASHINGTON, 1965

Rusty, Vincent

Rusty sat at his kitchen table, reading from a book about falcons, hawks and condors, Schorl curled comfortably on his lap. This book was not from the library; it was one of two he travelled with, the other about minerals, reminding him of the gypsum mine where his father had been caretaker, and of the private hoard of rocks left behind when he'd fled. He closed the book a moment, marking his place with a finger, wondering why he was still so drawn to the great predators, the scavengers. Then he snorted. Oh, I think you know, he said to himself.

At last, he shut the book, then closed his eyes, stroking Schorl absent-mindedly behind his ears. A few minutes later he sighed, an exhalation almost as deep as when he'd buried Burgundy. It was final. He needed to do it, didn't he?

It was raining when—the very next day—he made the short drive to North Thirteenth Street. The parking lot was paved and new, the administration building reminding him a lot of high school. Vincent Badger was being held in the East Complex, they'd told him, and the visit could last no longer than fifteen minutes. A surprise visit from an old friend was what he'd told the authorities. The surprise to him was that they'd bought it.

The room was clean and well lit, despite the absence of windows. The guard directed him to one of several picnic-style metal tables, then resumed his spot at the door, beside a second guard. Both cradled ominous-looking weapons.

Rusty's heart rate had been accelerating from the moment he'd entered the driveway, and it hadn't slowed yet. The body search hadn't flummoxed him, nor that they'd stripped away his pocket money for safekeeping. Nor had he been spooked by the heavily armed guards. But the very idea of prison was alarming. His first time inside, but not the first he'd worried about it.

A few minutes earlier, in the office, he'd said yes to the option of purchasing a soft drink card before they extracted his money, had bought a soda for himself and one for Badger. Now, both cans sat naked and sweating on the table, one in front of the empty space across from him. Coca Cola. Did he know if Vincent Badger liked Cokes? Hardly. He knew almost nothing. But he'd decided to give Badger the benefit of the doubt, hoping he'd turn out to be a standup guy. People can surprise you, he kept telling himself.

The far door opened and a small, slender man was led in. Wiry, hairy arms dangling from a short-sleeved orange jumpsuit. Slicked-back dark brown hair. Shoe-leather complexion. Small, intensely focused brown eyes. A year or two older than Maddie, perhaps? When he lowered himself to the bench, he did not look friendly.

Smiling, Rusty gestured toward the soda. Badger, poker-faced, ignored it.

"Who the hell are you?" he abruptly hissed, before Rusty had a chance to say hello. "Some goddamned reporter wants to know my life story? Or a tight-assed born-again craving to save my soul?" His gravelly voice Rusty found surprising, coming from someone of that age and build.

Rusty tried to keep his smile from freezing into caricature. "Neither, Mr. Badger. My name is Rusty Thomas, and…"

"You're the cocksucker's been fuckin' my wife."

With effort, Rusty managed to keep his features composed, not to lose his smile. Some grapevine.

"We've gotten close, Maddie and me, but, whatever you think, I'm not here to hassle you, Mr. Badger. I just came to ask, maybe it's time to think about letting Maddie go? She says she's been waiting a long while for you to sign those divorce papers. Now, I know you don't wanna see Maddie wastin' away if it's really over, right? If you care for her? She's a fine woman, who just wants to get on with the rest of her life."

The small man laughed. Snorted, rather.

"You got some fuckin' big ones, marchin' in here tellin' me what to do."

Rusty took a swallow of coke.

"I'm sorry if I've offended you, Mr. Badger. May I call you Vinnie?"

Silence. Rusty ran a knuckle back and forth along the bottom of his lip. "Look, if you were to be released tomorrow, what do you think would happen? Maddie would still feel the same."

"Fuck you, Asshole! You're a goddamn prick and you know it. A prick with a capital P."

At least he can spell, thought Rusty. "She says it's over, Mr. Badger. Why should you hold onto something that makes the woman you love so unhappy?"

This was not coming out right. He was blathering like a counselor. Or a social worker. He'd now decided this visit must be his worst idea in a decade. And he'd had some bad ideas!

He could feel heat rolling across the table in waves.

"What you need to do is stop fuckin' my wife, you understand? You stick your filthy johnson in her one more time, I'm gonna find a way to cut it off. Maddie is my wife.

The State of Washington said so, and still says so. I'm not divorcing her."

Then Washington State Prisoner #619004c (Rusty could read the number stenciled on the man's pocket) leaned across the table. "You think I can't fuck you up? You think those guards gonna stop me? Neither them nor the warden, nor God Almighty's gonna stop me once I make up my mind to do you."

He leaned closer. Rusty's mind flashed on a moment years ago when he'd held a varmint gun at the ready under his rain-slicker, safety off.

"Fuck her one more time and you're a dead man. You hear? I got friends on the outside. Don't think I can't get to you." Pressing in even further, he snarled. "And her, too."

For the first time, it was Rusty who broke eye contact. He looked at the wall, where windows ought to be, but weren't. The air around his ears was vibrating.

"Now *you* listen to *me*," he said quietly. The eyes he fastened on Badger were cold. "I don't answer to what you *feel*, but what you *do* is another matter. You touch one hair on Maddie's head, I'll blow a hole through your gut you can read a newspaper through."

He signaled a guard and, a moment later, was gone.

In the parking lot he sat a long time, watching raindrops accumulate and dissolve against his windshield.

He'd said, And her, too.

That's what he'd said. *And her, too.*

Chapter 10
MONTANA, 1970-71
Clayton

At nine each evening, like clockwork, Jake retired, and that was Clayton's opportunity to open his journal and spend an hour writing. One of those evenings, after closing his eyes and letting the warmth on his eyelids from the fireplace calm him for a minute or two, he picked up his pen and wrote: "Eagle in the Sky."

He thought a moment; crossed out "eagle" and then wrote, scratching out a line, pausing to think, changing a word here and there, a new poem. When he thought he finally had the version he wanted he re-copied it.

Hawk in the sky
turning

me on the ground
learning

up through the trees
yearning

hopeless, belly
churning

to measure the distance
between want
and accomplishment.
I rise off the ground
on my tippy-toes.

Leave the leaves,
Briefly

or think I do.

It's hard to know.

    He studied the poem a moment; crossed out the word "turning," wrote "perning" instead. To reference the Yeats poem. Better? Perhaps. Is "tippy-toes" too childish a phrase? Or, on the contrary, helpful? To show the child-like, naive notion of wanting to fly? A yearning for freedom? Is the poem any good?

Who knows? I don't use rhyme much, these days, he thought. But here…well…it just came out that way. Oh, hell. Maybe not done yet. He sighed. The poems had piled up over the years. He must have three hundred by now. Or more. Four journals full, all resident in his back-pack, swollen and rubber-banded, tattered from having been stuffed in and extracted from so many backpacks over so many years. And none published. But that issue would be addressed soon. He hoped.

He yawned, closed his journal, sought his bedroom, undressed and lay down, hoping—expecting—to sleep. But no sooner had he stretched out under the comforter, just as he could feel his body relaxing, a curious line emerged in his head. What was that about? He tried to dismiss it, but words suddenly surged up out of nowhere. Frowning, yet feeling almost possessed, he rose, opened his journal and wrote feverishly, without stopping

A bird perched on the rump of a horse
She rides, seeking goldfish,
Taking the sinewy motion of her mount
For her own.

Or else she flies, flees, tracing
A looping path through the aspens.
The watcher sees her disappear

On a curving trajectory behind a tree.

She does not reappear on the other side.
He is puzzled.
Can she change loops so fast?

He seeks the hiding tree and sleuths air only.
The watcher wonders where she has flown.
Perhaps there are goldfish there?
A horse whinnies from the underbrush, paws stone.

He looked at what he'd written. Where had that come from? Yet he knew, didn't he. He'd reversed it, however. It was he who had fled, not her.

Chapter 11

SOUTHEAST CITY, WASHINGTON, 1965

Rusty's Decision

Rusty was in the college library. A book, Mrs. Skorecky's choice, lay open on the table in front of him. He stared into space, mind fixed on a line he'd just read. *April is the cruelest month.*

When he'd first encountered the line, it had made no sense. He'd wondered then, was it supposed to? This was why he was living near the college in the first place. He needed some professionals, someone who'd studied and studied, to help him understand.

But now he was beginning to understand this poem, he thought. April is cruel because it ushers in a beauty that—once you've grown to love it—will, of certainty, be extinguished. Was that it? The end foretold from the beginning? The beginning must be viewed as pitiless because its death is certain, while in between the beginning and the end grows an attachment so sweet it hurts?

Two days earlier, when they'd last made love, Maddie was at her most passionate, he at his most withdrawn.

"What is it, love?" she'd asked afterwards. "What's bothering you? How can I help?"

He had smiled, kissed her, and shrugged. "Don't worry about it," was his rejoinder. "I'm working it out."

But was he? Could he? And how?

In the middle of August, he sat at his kitchen table, cat in his lap, feeling the weight of the world on his shoulders. Had this cat been Burgundy instead of Schorl, it might be rubbing its whiskers against Rusty's shirtfront, kneading his thighs, purring. But Schorl, still a kitten, was zonked. Sleepy, self-engrossed.

He felt bleak and bereft of hope, contemplating the letter he'd been writing to Maddie that lay open on his table. It was brief, yet he'd been at it for more than an hour now. Trying to explain how much she meant to him, trying to put into words how bereft he felt at this moment, how forlorn. Torn to pieces, in fact.

Because he'd decided he must move on. How to explain his devastation at this decision? He felt he needed to say that, whatever the hurt it caused him and—more important—however much it might hurt *her*, he must leave. And that this would likely mean he'd never see her again. Never speak to her. Never make love to her…again. Yet how could he possibly do that? How could he accept that it was over? That all this…sweetness, all the enriched self he felt *he* had become, must be cast off as if it had never been.

Once he'd thought to share all his passions and all his fears with Maddie. Tell her everything. All of it. *My God! Thirteen years*! How had he managed to tell no one in all this time? No one except…Alejandro.

So all morning he'd been pacing, stuffed with emotion yet feeling like a peanut shell after the nut has been removed. Measuring the bedroom. Circling the kitchen. Around and around the living room. Hoisting himself up on that still-dead stove, staring out the window at the yellow roses in his garden. Endlessly juggling choices and consequences, and in between, in pieces, sitting down to write the letter. Even now—pen poised above the page—he was considering do I tell her *why* I'm leaving. Should I include that? Or not?

Of course he wanted to. He ached to. Desperately.

But *no*, another part of him cautioned. The mine? The gun? The stupid cover-up? His doubts about himself as to whether he was, might be…instinctively…a killer?

No. Don't go there, he told himself. Pandora's box.

I'm not afraid of him, Maddie, he thought, but did not write. It's what I might do to him should he come after me that gives me pause. Or, for certain, if he tried to harm you. And maybe…just maybe…if I leave, he will not do you harm. It's my absence that I hope will prevent that.

He felt the pen twitch in his fingers, a signal to resume writing. In the end, he decided to leave out the explanation altogether. His burden. Keep it that way.

Hastily he scrawled that he was leaving Schorl behind for her to remember him by, that he hoped she wouldn't mind taking care of him.

Give Sammy a hug for me, he wrote finally, and ended, *All my love.* Then wrote it again. And a third time. *All my love, Rusty.*

He closed his eyes a moment, trying to steady his breathing. Finally, summoning all his will, he rose, unloaded Schorl onto the table, folded his letter, tucked it in the envelope.

She had a key. He knew she would let herself in tomorrow, to wait for him, knew she would find the note. He swiveled his head around on his shoulders to loosen his neck muscles. As he did so, he caught sight of the Model 24 in the corner. Another decision. Or was it already made? Was he right to leave it? There, perhaps, was the largest question of all. During the past week, without telling her anything about the gun except that he'd once hunted small varmints, he'd taken her out shooting. Set up tin cans in the foothills. Showed her how to use the gun. Which the shotgun part, which the rifle. How to load each, how to discharge each. She knows now, he reassured himself. But still.

The hand that grasped the envelope trembled.

He paused again. Through the kitchen window, he could see golden-crested wrens fluttering around the lone sycamore across the street.

I can't see mountains from here, he thought, but I know they are there. Good. Okay. I need sparrow-hawks now, and falcons. Maybe I can spot a condor again? There has to be an upside somewhere.

Left to his own devices, Schorl was now prancing across the tabletop. Perhaps he imagined himself a lion, this stretch of oilcloth his veldt. He sniffed here, sniffed there, sought the ideal spot to continue his nap. Rusty gently brushed the cat off the envelope, fished out the letter and crossed out a line. He wrote a quick PS: "Changed my mind. Took the cat. Love you, Rusty."

He glanced once more at the gun in the corner, stuffed but did not seal the envelope, dropped the house keys on the table, swept the kitten off the oilcloth and snatched up the valise he'd packed earlier, which included the two books he carried everywhere. Then he took a deep breath and left, closing the door firmly behind him.

CHAPTER 12

ALASKA, 1968

CHRIS & THE OLD POET

CHRIS STUDIED HIS surroundings with the curious eye of an outdoorsman who'd spent very little time in hotel rooms. The room was large, part of a suite in fact, and it's most striking feature—to him at least, as he sat in a straight-backed chair only a few feet away—was the sizable oak desk with a matching swivel chair before it and three enormous piles of books, in a disarray he found somehow pleasing. He'd been in very few hotel rooms, none at all of this size.

But he couldn't take his eyes off those books. Old, mostly, tattered and scuffed, some. Perhaps their fascination came from the fact that they suggested a kind of wealth—not of money, what did he know of money?—but of ideas and inspiration. Though it might also have been, perhaps—he smiled when he thought this—because it made him wonder whether the man brought his whole library with him when he traveled? Chris knew for a fact—well, it had been stated on the flyer he'd seen outside the bookshop—that the well-known poet lived in New York City, about as far from Anchorage as you could get .

His senses had been sharpened by apprehension. How daring it now seemed to propose a one-on-one conversation with a celebrated poet! He'd never done anything remotely like this.. A few minutes earlier he'd been served a cup of coffee by the poet's wife, a petite, attractive older woman with bobbed grey hair, whom he found charmingly fussy and attentive.

She'd swept into the room with a welcoming smile and dancing eyes that connected immediately to you. Her manner had called to mind someone he'd known once, a friendly librarian he'd met in a different town. But remembering *that* town gave birth to another memory—Lord help us!—of a younger woman, someone from the same small city with whom he'd been way more than casually connected, and whose memory he now tried to banish as quickly as it had surfaced, as he'd done for some three years. The effort echoed through his body. He closed his eyes. Didn't happen! Didn't happen! He could not afford to think of her.

Once he'd cleared his mind, he became suddenly

agitated. When was this famous poet going to show? Was this some kind of fever dream? He closed his eyes again.

And when he opened them, the Old Poet stood before him as if transported there by magic.

"Asleep already?" the man asked, with a hint of a smile. "I usually take my naps a little later than this."

Chris blushed deeply, casting around wildly for what he'd practiced as his opening line.

He'd met the man briefly the previous evening, had stumbled onto awareness of the reading through a flyer in the window, which announced that a well-known poet—and editor of poets—was in town just for this one evening. Or perhaps it was one of a series; Chris hadn't read that carefully. He'd simply made a spur of the moment decision to go.

It was early June, two weeks to the Summer Solstice Festival, when the sun was still out almost twenty hours a day. He'd no plans to see the festival, though he could imagine it would be filled with protests about the Vietnam War. But he'd taken his earnings from the logging camp where he'd been working for a while and made his way back to Anchorage. Since he'd been planning to leave the city the very next day to embark upon the trip south, his change of plans in front of the bookstore had been quite sudden. Then he'd not only attended the reading that evening but afterwards bought the book of poems the poet was selling, taking care to position himself at the tail end of the line of purchasers.

When the moment came for the man's signature, he'd not only asked for the autograph but, with his heart in his throat, also wondered whether he might meet with the fine gentleman a few minutes the following day to discuss the craft of poetry? He described himself as an untrained wannabe, a blank-slate, a novice who craved some expert advice.

The Old Poet had wrinkled his brow at first, cocked his head to one side, glanced at his watch, looked in the direction of the bookstore owner, already beginning to clear away the unsold books and break down the tables and chairs set up for the reading. Then he'd turned back and said, smiling, "Why, of course."

And now?

"Oh, no! Sorry, sir. I just . . I only…"

But before he could get any further, the Old Poet reached out and greeted Chris by pumping the younger man's hand with both of his then settling himself in his chair.

"Well, young man," he said. "I believe you said you wanted to talk poetry."

Chris swallowed, hoping not to betray his jitters but certain it showed. He felt he'd like to dissolve into the half-cup of coffee he'd managed a moment ago to lower to the rug.

"Uh, yes sir, that's right," he said. "I've not had any formal training. I mean, none at all. Never even quite finished high school. But a friend got me started reading poetry ten or twelve years ago and I was so fascinated—so seized by it, you might say—that I've been trying to write poems ever since."

"Seized, you say!" said the Old Poet, and smiled again. "Well, there are worse things than being seized, I suppose."

Folding his hands and settling farther into his chair, he asked what poets Chris liked. His watery eyes, set amidst old wrinkles but still a riveting cobalt blue, seemed to smile almost as deeply as his mouth did. His white hair was cut long and wavy.

Chris cleared his throat. "Well, I like these, for sure," he said, indicating the book in his lap he'd bought the previous evening. "Though I'm sorry to say I haven't had a very long acquaintance with your work. I just…well… umm…let's see…." He cleared his throat. "I guess W. H. Auden is someone I enjoy. And admire. Very much so."

The Old Poet nodded in approval. "Good choice."

"The first poets I started reading were Dylan Thomas and T. S. Eliot. Oh! Excuse me! That's not true. The first poet I actually became acquainted with was Lorca."

"Lorca! My word! That's certainly unusual. You're telling me you've read Garcia Lorca?"

"Why, yes sir. Mostly in Spanish. I mean, I can't say I'm widely acquainted with his work, but I am aware of some beautiful poems, which I try as best I can to translate into English."

"Hah! So you know Spanish then?"

"A little. The friend I mentioned was Mexican. His father was a poet and he carried around a book of Lorca's poems which I…inherited."

The Old Poet cocked his head to the side and leaned closer. "Fascinating! So, tell me. Who else do you like?"

"Uh…Edward Arlington Robinson, I guess. He's really something, I think. Old fashioned these days, maybe, but still. I especially like his longer poems. And maybe A. E. Houseman? The English fellow?"

The poet chuckled and nodded his head.

"Yes, good. Good. But still, except for Auden, of course, none of these guys are around these days. Anybody else? How about Howard Nemerov? Ever heard of him?"

"I don't think so."

"Well, I recommend him. You should know these younger guys, the ones writing now. Theodore Roethke, Richard Wilbur, Randall Jarrell, James Dickey."

Chris had slipped the pen from his shirt pocket and was busy writing names in a black notebook he'd held underneath his copy of the poet's book.

"Let's see," the poet continued. "Robert Lowell, of course. And women, too…Elizabeth Bishop, for example. Muriel Rukeyser. Denise Levertov. Oh, there are lots of good ones. But keep your eye on Howard Nemerov."

Chris nodded while feverishly trying to record all these names.

The old poet added a few more names for good measure. Then he grew quiet and stared at Chris intently as he wrote.

"Tell me. In your notebook there," he said at last. "You have poems of your own?"

"Oh, sure. Yes sir. I do."

"May I see them?"

Chris swallowed and extended the notebook, trying to keep his hand from shaking. This was the point, wasn't it? Of course it was.

The Old Poet began to examine the notebook. Slowly, at a measured pace, flicking pages, rustling through, sometimes slowing to a stop, frequently chuckling to himself. Occasionally he punctuated the air with a "hmph" or a "hmm" or muttered a bit, advancing onto a following page with a noisy rustle.

Twice Chris saw him frown and bounce his head sideways. Occasionally he made noises deep in his throat that put Chris's teeth on edge. Once he looked off into the distance, pondering. Every once in a while he smiled and nodded his head.

Finally, after ten or fifteen minutes, he closed the book, handed it back, and smiled.

"Well, keep at it, lad," he said. "Just keep at it. You've a good eye and a steady hand."

He paused and looked off into the distance again. Or maybe at the blue curtains that were rustling in the breeze coming through the half-opened window. Chris had not even noticed the breeze until now.

"Keep listening and keep looking at things," he said. "Observation is important, and I think you have a good instinct for that. Your love for birds and trees and minerals and things—for nature, in a word—is finely honed. It's special. Yes sir, keep using that."

"Thank you, sir! That's very kind of you to say. I always…"

The old man plowed on, paying scant attention to Chris's interruption.

"Just an observation, young man. Now, allow me to continue. As I said, you should listen to the sounds around you, but—and this is important—attend as well to the sounds of human speech."

Chris swallowed but stayed silent, fearful of interrupting the discourse and, at the same time, eager to hear whatever advice was forthcoming.

"Poems, after all, like other forms of writing, evolved from spoken tales—long before things got written down. And how the spoken language sounds, how the words sound when they're brought into contact with one another, is important. Crucial, in fact. It may be a deeper meaning you're striving for, most of the time, but it won't work if it's *just* meaning."

He looked away again for a moment, then moved his arms as if gathering something in. A small cloud, perhaps? Chris watched, fascinated, half-holding his breath, wondering if this was a moment when he could ask a question. But then, the poet smiled at him, warmly, looked deep into his eyes and said, "It's what resonates and signifies at the same time. The magic lies in how that meaning is brought to fruition, or even into being, by the music of the words."

Then the older man simply handed the notebook back to his guest and rose abruptly, looking suddenly distracted and vague, agitated. "I'm sorry, now, my young friend. Mr. Jenkins, is it?"

"Yes sir. Chris, sir."

"Yes, yes. Well. Now, Chris, I have other stuff I must attend to. So, thank you for coming, Mr. Jekyll. Uh, Jenkins. Sorry, sorry. Thank you for showing me your poems. An honor."

He reached out, did a brief bow, then surrounded Chris's hands, both of them, including the notebook and pen as well since that could not be avoided, and pumped the whole shebang once, ending on the down-stroke.

"Now I must run. Thank you again. Goodbye."

He disappeared into the next room.

A few heartbeats later, Chris stood outside the suite, leaning back against the door, breathing deeply. He'd waited a moment after the old poet's departure, then let himself out, since no one had come to show him the door. His thoughts lingered a moment on the brusque end to the audience. Were all poets like that? What soon engulfed him, however, was the altogether astonishing warmth of his welcome. By such a well-known, important poet. How much time the old gent had given him! Plus, he'd actually read some of his poems! And even liked them—a few of them, at least.

Wow! he said to himself, as he made his way down the stairs and out into the afternoon sunlight.

He felt lightheaded, almost ready to fly. Most of all, as he wandered down the street, he kept remembering the old man's words at the very end. How meaning is brought into being by the music of the words.

Of course, it could be that's what he says to all aspiring writers, Chris thought. Or maybe not. In any event, he decided, those words might be worth a lifetime of poetry classes. In any case, they're all I'm likely to get. If I can just remember his words!

It was cool on the street and breezy. A few puffy cumulus clouds, looking for all the world like the armful Chris imagined the old man had been reaching for, bounced the light out of the sky onto the sidewalk. That light would be around for many more hours he knew. But as he made his way toward the restaurant where he'd decided to have lunch he found his mind returning again and again to the messages he had taken away from his meeting with the poet.

"Not just meaning," he whispered to himself, willing the words he had heard the old man utter to be indelibly etched on his mind. "Not just meaning," he reiterated. "But the music. The magic."

CHAPTER 13

MONTANA, 1970-71

Clayton, Angie, Maddie

It was snowing lightly as Clayton left Morning Noon & Night, having delivered the milk the restaurant regularly bought from Henderson's farm. He began walking toward where he'd parked the pickup, trying to decide whether he could afford to spend a half-hour in the library, when a shout from behind brought him up short.

"Johnny! Is that you!"

A chilling panic. He recognized the voice. After a split second's hesitation, he turned.

"Angie! My God! What on earth are you doing here?"

"John Liverpool! My goodness! Long time no see, fella! And may I ask you the same thing?" She looked around. "What's this burg called anyway?"

Many times he had pondered: In this game I am

running, this life I am trying to live, this course I have willy-nilly put myself on, what is my worst nightmare? The answer always the same: the arrival of someone who knew him by another name. The threat that, with the slightest touch, his row of carefully arranged dominoes, arrayed like uniformed soldiers across a table, might come tumbling down.

He put his game face on. "Hey, welcome to Rolling Hills, Montana. Actually, it's a nice town."

"You live here?"

"Out of town a ways. Work for a farmer. Today I was delivering some stuff to town." He glanced around quickly, saw no one on the street, tried to disguise his sense of relief.

"Wow!" Her smile was broad. "I never thought I'd see *you* again! What's it been? Ten years?"

He forced a grin, raised his eyebrows, looked down, looked up again.

"Something like that. Good Lord, Angie! What brings you to these parts?"

She looked at him and paused. She still knew how to lock in eye contact, he thought.

"Long story, but…say? Is there some place besides this snowy sidewalk we can talk? I stopped to get something to eat. That's my car back there." She motioned over her shoulder. Even before he looked he was sure it would be a Cadillac. Nor was he surprised that it was red.

Angelina Dobbs. My goodness. Ten years ago and many

miles away. He could swear she hadn't changed. Cheeks a little fuller perhaps. Were her lashes even longer? In any event, just as stunning. Clayton, breaking eye contact only for a moment, glanced around again, hoping not to betray the desperation that had overwhelmed him.

"Why, of course! I need to get back to the farm soon, but I've certainly got time for a cup of coffee with an old friend. Matter of fact, we're right in front of the best place in town to eat. Shall we?"

He guided her into the café, steering her to a corner booth, waving distractedly at Martin Randall, to whom he had just delivered two aluminum canisters of milk. Martin approached with menus and took their orders, flashing Clayton a private look that managed to be both smutty and impressed.

"So!" Clayton said, as Martin headed back to the kitchen. "What brings you to my neck of the woods, young lady?"

"And it really is the woods, isn't it? What an out-of-the-way place! Well, buddy! I'm on my way to New York! From Seattle. On the map, this looked like a good route." She paused. That smile again.

"I've been accepted into the Actor's Studio!" she said, with such breath and eagerness that Clayton tried to remember if he'd heard the name. It didn't matter; her tone conveyed its importance.

"Hey, that's super! Exciting! So you're still planning to become an actress!"

Wasn't she always? She'd been eighteen the spring they'd met, about to graduate high school. And he was twenty-two, working in the Eureka vicinity as a logger. With his first time off in months, he'd come down from the hills east of Humboldt Bay to where that small lumber and fishing town stretched out along the strand. When he'd pondered his choices and decided to attend a performance of the Eureka Community Theater's production of *Little Mary Sunshine*, he found her playing the title role. There'd been nothing in the program that identified her as his boss's daughter. His big boss, the lumber impresario, Clarence Dobbs.

That was 1960. It was spring. She was beautiful. Her voice and looks had enthralled him. Slapped him silly. Normally shy and committed to keeping a low profile, he'd felt so addled yet energized at the sight of her that he'd waited in lovesick dread in the parking lot outside the theatre, and then—with a genius for persuasion he'd never known he had—managed to wrest her away from two high school girlfriends—fellow actors, also in the play—who'd clearly planned to drive her home.

At that point he'd still had his Essex, of course, still a year before he sold it to a collector. Its cushy leather back seat provided the location, before the evening was out, for a torrid *pas de deux* in which Angela's expensive panties wound up dangling from a shapely ankle, while a nonplussed Clayton—whom she knew as John—needed to withdraw at the very last minute because he hadn't thought to bring a condom. The mess had embarrassed him but to her, seemed only to amuse. Clearly, not her first time.

An hour later he drove her home to discover she lived on a landscaped hillside in the middle of Eureka in a huge Victorian built by her grandfather and known locally as the Dobbs Mansion.

"Already *am* an actress, Buster," she said, puncturing his reverie. "Left Eureka to study theater arts at the University of Washington. After I graduated, I appeared pretty often in productions in Seattle. My reputation grew. Small parts became bigger ones. You know the drill."

He knew nothing of the drill but raised his eyebrows and continued to smile.

"Once, by request, I appeared in the Little Theatre of that stuffy little town, Southeast City. *The Lady's Not for Burning*. You ever in Southeast City?"

He looked away. "Passed through it once, I believe. A tad larger than Eureka, isn't it?"

"Oh, you were always such a *small town boy*, Johnny. Anyway, I have lots of acting creds in Seattle now. It's not stretching a point to say, I'm *quite* famous there."

He remembered that drive. That confidence. That… let's face it…condescension. He'd used "narcissistic" in a poem once. The word jumped into his brain now.

"Anyway, now that I've got experience, I'm ready for the big time. On my way to the Big Apple, fella! One day you'll come to the Great White Way and see my name in lights! Or maybe…." She batted her eyelashes. "You'll catch me in a movie."

"My, my! How exciting! And to think I knew you when." Clayton glanced out the window. The street was still clear.

A long pause ensued while she ate her scrambled eggs and toast and he drank his fourth cup of coffee of the day. His dread eased a little.

When she was finished with her meal she dabbed her lips with a napkin, pushed her plate aside, cast him a searching look.

Those big eyes. The ink-black hair, in ringlets, the thin nose, the patrician face.

"So what happened, John? Something I did? You disappeared so quickly, it was like…. I was kind of smitten with you, you know? Over it now, of course. Hell, I've already been married *and* divorced. Annulled, really. But still, I'm curious."

He searched his mind desperately for an answer, one that wouldn't implicate, but before he could speak, she laughed, snared his eyes again. "We had some good times, didn't we, John?"

He colored slightly. "Ah! We certainly did, Angie. That we did."

She reached across the table and brushed the top of his hands with her manicured nails. The same shade of red as her car. Coincidence? Nah. "You were an energetic guy in the back of that grand old car! Oooh, Johnny!"

He blushed more and withdrew his hands, trying to disguise his unease with a laugh. He could not deny a quiver of arousal, but he could also feel, again, the approach of panic.

He counted himself lucky that she'd never found out—back in Eureka—how he made his living or, more important, who his big boss was. Their affair *and* his job would have been over like a thunderclap had her father found out. And the risk to him wouldn't have ended there. So, after a while, he'd simply steered clear of her.

"Well," she said. "I guess I'd better be on my way. Walk me out, sport?"

The snow had stopped. A couple strolled the sidewalk on the opposite side of the street. No one Clayton knew, thank God.

When they reached her car, he opened the door for her, cursing himself for his valet mentality.

"Well, so long, Angie. Knock 'em dead in New York! Looks like Hollywood's a sure thing for you. What amazing luck running into you here! What are the chances, hey? Wow! Be good to yourself, okay?"

Then, before he knew what was happening, she kissed him. He drew back as soon as he thought it not insulting, glanced at her diamond-encrusted watch. A present from her doting father?

"Too bad I don't have a little more time, hey?" She smiled coquettishly. "Otherwise…"

"Get outta here, girl! Before we do something we'll both be sorry for. Seriously, it was really, really good to see you again, Angie. Really. Listen! Have a great life in New York! And wherever else your star takes you."

She started the engine, smiling as she pulled away. He held his own smile until the Cadillac was safely down the road, waving, then stood there in the middle of the street and shook his head. Damn. *That* was a close call.

Was it over? Through the plate glass window, he noticed Martin Randall leering at him. Jittery though he was, Clayton decided to risk yet another cup of coffee.

"Some babe, Clayton," said Martin, a moment later, tweaking his handlebar moustache. "Old flame?"

"Well, yes, as a matter of fact," said Clayton. "Many years ago."

"I wanted to ask…didn't I hear her call you Johnny?"

His mind churned. "Why, yes! That's right! Don't use my middle name much these days. Clayton John Poole, at your service."

He hoped that had put an end to it.

On the drive back to the farm his mind was a tangle of competing thoughts and overlapping images. Focused at first on Angelina, mainly how relieved he was to be rid of her. Interspersed, unavoidably, with provocative memories. How stunning the attraction he'd felt for her at that first sighting! Which he could admit to now that she was safely gone.

But then images of Maddie rose from the deep to eclipse those of Angie—Maddie in only her nylons on their first evening together, when she swung aside the door of her trailer. Maddie in his bed in the early afternoon, stroking the kitten she'd helped him find to replace Burgundy. Maddie hugging him so tightly in her mother's house in Yakima, right after they'd finished putting her son to bed.

My God! He hadn't slept with anyone since Maddie. No one. Over many miles and what seemed endless years. There'd been opportunities, for sure, but it was a line he couldn't bring himself to cross.

Not that it had been totally a conscious decision, exactly. What was conscious, what was definitely deliberate, was his determination to forget. His *need* to forget. And there was that ever-present fear, that conviction that his own stupidity had screwed things up so dreadfully with the only woman he'd ever truly loved.

He'd been haunted by those memories for years—but he'd always managed to show them the door, dismissing each one as it rose to the surface with a phrase such as: "what can't be, can't be" or "that way lies melancholy," or some such anodyne. But now—on this drive back to the farm—they ambushed him, ravaged him. Refused to leave.

The moments with Angelina certainly *were* intense, he remembered—but with Maddie it had been different. There was ardor, but also an ease. A value. An admiration. And always a hint that— in the future—perhaps a shared life? In short, he'd loved Maddie. Desperately. God help him, he still did.

He longed for her now. He smiled when he recalled how she'd given up smoking for him, on the spot, in minutes, and a moment later lain her head on his shoulder. "My protector," she'd called him. And wasn't that, in the end, why he'd left? Hoping to protect her by simply removing himself from the equation?

He sighed. So hard, still, to remember that he'd relinquished that relationship of his own free will! Yet, not free, really. *No!* Not free!

"For *HER*," he said out loud to himself now, repeating it over and over under his breath. "I did it for her. In the hope of making her safer."

So he'd said at the time and so he still believed. He remembered thinking that if to protect her, he'd been led to shoot someone and had then been captured by the prison system, she'd have wound up no better off than before. Worse, in fact. Once again, her "man" would be in lockup, obliterating all possibility of a life together.

That was how he'd seen it then. And now? Had anything changed?

All the way back to the farm, such thoughts assailed

him. When he reached the spot where he usually parked the pickup, he felt a wreck. He sat for a long while in the truck's cab. Which recalled to him another time he'd paused for long moments in a pickup, in the rain. In a prison parking lot.

He remained locked into a torpor, hardly moving, gripping the wheel as if it were a life raft, until the sun vanished behind the western mountains, and he heard the cows lowing, begging to be milked.

Chapter 14

MONTANA 1970-71

Clayton, Frank

And just like that, winter was gone. For months, whether on snowshoes through the deep drifts or driving into town in the farm's pickup, Clayton had become familiar with the townspeople as well as the stores and streets of Rolling Hills. Which was rather his hope when he launched his journey across the Bitterroots the previous fall. His major hope. Today, as he strolled down Main Street on the first day of spring, an awkward bundle under his arm, he found himself looking at each shop with the pleasure of a familiar acquaintance.

Here was the general store, called *Osgoods*. After Horace Osgood, the owner. Osgood was not a talkative man, but friendly enough. He wore a visored cap and garters on his sleeves and—it was rumored—ran a small poker game every Saturday night in the back room. Clayton caught Horace's eye as he passed the large picture window. Shifting the bundle he was carrying to his left arm, he waved. It was answered with a broad smile.

Next was *StopN'Shop*, the grocery store, whose merchandise somewhat overlapped with Osgoods, but they seemed to have been easily coexisting rivals for thirty years or more. On the corner of Main Street and Deuteronomy.

Deuteronomy! That name slayed Clayton. What clutch of pioneering evangelicals, he wondered, had managed to name that street? He'd been to this corner grocery often enough, buying victuals for both himself and the Hendersons, and wondered now why he'd never asked that question. He also wondered how they'd managed to keep such a wide selection of fresh, top-quality meats in stock? Well, no doubt that was partly because the meat was slaughtered and dressed locally. Much of it wasn't even parceled out in two or three-pound packages, in fact; you could easily ask for a side of beef or a whole mutton. And the staff could have told you the farm that raised the animal, if you'd an inclination to ask. The staff of *StopN'Shop* was always welcoming, he knew, except for one sullen high-school age cashier, whose employment was, Clayton imagined, a favor to the boy's parents.

In the next block he passed the café he knew so well by now. He saluted Martin through the window, already behind the counter at this hour. And, recalling his mid-winter encounter with Angie, he could only hope the man would remember to keep his mouth shut. *If he doesn't, and I need to leave town, I'll rip off his handlebar moustache before I go.* He chortled to himself. *Of course he wouldn't. Martin was a friend.*

Still walking, he passed the barber shop, where he'd had his hair cut and beard trimmed twice this winter. *What was the barber's name, now? Leonard? No, Lester.* Clayton smiled and nodded on his way past the candy-cane barber's pole.

This is a friendly town, he thought. *A nice town.* He'd never been drawn to cities, though only in the large municipalities was it possible to identify those who might provide, for a price, a forged driver's license, with whatever name and birth date, you desired. That had proved useful, if expensive.

It was also his experience that not all towns were equally friendly. Lewiston, Idaho, for one. And Ellensburg, Washington. Of course all towns had their grouches and curmudgeons, he supposed. And crazies. Certainly even here there were people who might get panicked enough to dash into the snow in cold weather in a thin dress and house-slippers. And get their ankle caught in a bear trap. *I didn't make that up.*

He slowed his pace. Most important, he said to himself, what very few small towns *did* have, was an establishment like the one he had finally arrived at. He drew up before a building he'd not had the courage to seek out until this moment, even though it was the destination he'd aimed at from the first, in that long hike across the Bitterroots.

He felt his heart beating loud and fast, like an impatient small-deeds knight pounding on the door of a medieval castle. The package under his arm? His poetry. Five journals full. Many years of writing, crossing out, ripping up, revising—all re-copied here. His heart was in these poems. His soul, it felt like. He pushed open the entrance to a weekly newspaper with serious aspirations, *The Rolling Hills Reporter*.

Inside, a long counter. A young girl—short, dark hair, a little on the plump side—sat behind a large oak desk in the middle of a huge, rectangular space. She was positioned midway between the counter and a back wall that led, by the look of things, into two offices, each with the sort of rippling, stippled windows you might find in a bank, behind which the Manager, or the Assistant Manager, resided. Both doors were closed.

To Clayton, the young girl's desk, given the size of the place, seemed isolated. Why were there not other desks? Wasn't this a busy place? The left side of the room, he noticed, opened onto another space, separated by a sliding door, which was, at this minute, open; a glance showed it to be taken up by a good-sized printing press. And immediately before him was a counter-top strewn with overlapping copies of newspapers. Issues of *The Rolling*

Hills Reporter were arranged in two orderly piles at each end. And the latest issues of other newspapers were strung out along the counter. *The New York Times*, *The Chicago Daily Tribune*, *The St. Louis Post-Dispatch*, *The Minneapolis Star-Ledger*. All heavy hitters, he knew. Suddenly, his observations were brought up short by the girl's question. She'd had to ask it a second time.

"May I *help* you?"

"Oh! Sorry!" Clayton smiled. "Is the editor around? I'd like to speak to him." He made a show of flipping open the front page of *The Reporter*, scanning the masthead deliberately. "Mr. Bascombe, am I right?"

Why such an act? Nerves? Clayton chided himself for this pretense of ignorance. He knew who Frank Bascombe was, and how *The Rolling Hills Reporter* was viewed. He'd come across the newspaper two years earlier, a library copy in a different state. And with the help of the librarian, done some research. Learned how the independently wealthy Bascombe—a Journalism graduate at Northwestern University—had decided to start a newspaper that he could put his own stamp on. In a place where he would not be hindered or restrained.

So Bascombe had come west to Montana, found this community, bought a building and started from scratch. Apparently—this is what Clayton had dug up—Bascombe was an admirer of Upton Sinclair, Lincoln Steffens, Ida Tarbell and other muckraking stars of the past. And in the ten years since he'd been in operation, the fame of Bascombe's paper—though small and only a weekly—had spread. And that was the place Clayton had decided he needed to be.

"Right you are," said the girl. "Let me see if he's busy." She pushed a button on her intercom. "Mr. Bascombe? A gentleman to see you."

A gentleman, thought Clayton. Well, that was a first!

A minute later, Frank Bascombe emerged from his office and crossed to where Clayton stood. He was a small man who wore khakis and a white shirt, sleeves rolled up to the elbows. Hair thin and white, gathered around a prominent widow's peak like filaments of fine thread. Despite the hair, Clayton judged him to be in his mid-fifties.

"Frank Bascombe," he said, extending his hand. "How can I help?" A minute later, at the editor's beckoning, they were in his office.

Clayton cleared his throat. "I don't know whether you've ever published poetry," he began, squirming a bit. "But I've written quite a few, which I think—which I hope—are pretty good, and I was hoping you might be able to print some of them. Over time, of course. Assuming you find them acceptable."

Bascombe scratched at the back of his head. "Poems, you say? Well, well." He leaned back in his chair. "Funny you should mention it. I've been thinking about that very thing, believe it or not. A 'poem of the week' column.

Originals, you understand, not stuff already printed elsewhere. Been in my head for a while now, but I've been too busy to consider it. Plus nobody to help out with something like that. Listen, are you local? Don't lie to me, son, I think I'd know."

"Of course you would," Clayton smiled. "You probably know everything that goes on in this town."

"We try."

After that day, during which Clayton had showed him a few poems and the editor had clucked over them excitedly and agreed to print them, one each week, starting with the very next issue, Clayton found himself returning to *The Rolling Hills Reporter* every afternoon that circumstances permitted. Given that Marjorie was walking with a cane by now, and could make tea for herself, he felt no obligation to continue their afternoon visits. When they did have tea together Clayton became as animated and talkative as he'd earlier been mostly a listener. The focus of his attention had shifted from farm to town and his excitement showed.

Although he'd revealed very little about his personal life, when the editor's probing ways discovered the circumstances of Clayton's arrival in the area—the bear-trap and what he thought of as a remarkable act of heroism—his eyebrows jumped. "The hell you say! Now there's something I didn't know. Say, do you write other things besides poetry? I wouldn't mind a story about Ms. Henderson and the bear trap. Water under the bridge by now, hardly up-to-the-minute news, but still, a good feature. And nobody would know more than you, right? We could use the help, Mr. Poole, if you were so inclined. Might even pay you some. Not much, but something."

Clayton brightened. "That's sort of what I was hoping for, to be honest. I'm a greenhorn at journalism, of course, but I wouldn't mind giving it a try. Although—" He frowned. "I don't know about that particular story. I'm not one to give away private confidences."

Frank Bascombe smiled. "Believe it or not, I understand, Mr. Poole. You've hit upon the inevitable dilemma of the small-town reporter: how much do you tell? Most times the people who *make* the news shouldn't be *writing* about it. Tell you what, though. Why don't you write me such a piece anyway? Make a stab at it: simple and short. Don't include what feels like a private confidence. Just who-what-when-where-why. Get it? Or how, depending. You're not reporting on a nuclear disaster, for heaven's sake! Then show it to me and I'll critique it. Teach you the basics."

He grinned and continued.

"I own this newspaper as well as edit and print it, Mr. Poole. One man band, so to speak. Studied at the Medill School of Journalism at Northwestern, then came west and began this paper twenty years ago. Don't make much money; some months I lose, in fact, but I love it. It's in my blood. And within reason, I try to pay well enough for stories I don't generate on my own."

The editor's grin was non-stop as his arm swept out in a wide flourish.

"Those newspapers you see on the counter out there? We subscribe to major papers from all over. A big part of our budget! You can certainly keep current if you're interested. A library, if you will, of current events. Across the country, around the world. We also have a morgue of other small-town newspapers in this part of the country. The Pacific Northwest. Most of them, stretching back over the twenty years since I began *The Rolling Hills Reporter*.

"Now, you know Abby out there. She's my only full-time employee. Just finishing high school. Coupla months, she'll be gone. Getting married and flitting off to Gainesville, in Florida. What a change that will be, eh? Lived here all her life, since she was born. But that's how it works, isn't it? People grow, people change, circumstances change, countries change. Nothing stands still, Mr. Poole. Am I right?"

Chapter 15
MONTANA 1970-71
CLAYTON, MARJORIE, FRANK

A MONTH PASSED. LATE at night, in the middle of May, Clayton woke to the noise of furious voices, followed by a door being slammed, or was it a pistol shot? He scrambled out of bed, slipped on his pants and, barefoot and shirtless, trotted to the front of the house.

A car squatted aslant the gravel driveway, driver-side door ajar, headlamps illuminating figures on the porch steps. Rain was falling and a hatless man stood in his shirt sleeves halfway between the car and the house, waving his arms wildly and shouting. He'd been there long enough to become quite wet. No sign of a gun at this point. Approaching the porch, Clayton saw Jake standing there, a woman he had never seen before clinging to him, weeping. He noticed Marjorie at the back of the porch, looking horrified. Quickly he pushed past her to join Jake on the steps.

"Damaged goods!" he heard the stranger yell. "Ya hear me? A fucking whore! You can keep your goddamned daughter, you got that? I never want to see that bitch again."

The man was clearly drunk. Although he'd never met him, Clayton understood that this was Thomas Gilroy, the husband of Jake's daughter, Lynette.

"Get the hell off my property!" Jake yelled at Gilroy. In the glare of the headlights Clayton could see the farmer's jaw muscles twitching. "I never want to see your sorry bones in this state again, you jackass!"

Although several yards away, the man made a lurching, threatening move toward Jake, then stopped, noticing Clayton for the first time.

"Who the hell are *you*!" he yelled, his voice hoarse from all his shouting. He blinked and staggered, then righted himself.

"None of your goddamned business who he is!" Jake shouted back. "He's my hired hand, you sick fool! Now just get outta here before I clock your sorry ass." He passed his daughter into Clayton's arms and began to strip off his belt.

Clayton put a hand on Jake's shoulder, though he never took his eyes off the eyes of the man in the rain. "Never mind, Jake," he said calmly. His tone was quiet but arresting. "The gentleman was just leaving. Let him go."

A fierce glare from Gilroy, who stood in the rain a

moment longer, breathing heavily, rivers streaming down his face, conflicting impulses flitting across it. Finally, he stumbled back toward the open door of his car, mumbling under his breath. "Keep her!" he shouted again. "Goddamn whore. Keep her." He vanished into the car, slammed the door on the second try. The vehicle spun around and fishtailed down the driveway, spewing gravel.

Jake's daughter had wound her arms so desperately around him that he had to pry her away to return her to her father, where she broke down once again, sobbing into his chest. Giving Jake's shoulder a final squeeze, Clayton turned back toward the doorway. As he passed Marjorie, he saw her studying him. He raised his eyebrows, shrugged and shook his head before returning to his room. His look said: You are family; I'm not needed here.

In bed, however, fingers laced behind his head, he stared at the stilled ceiling fan. Sleep eluded him. His mind drifted from memory to memory, mostly about violence of one sort or another. One emerged in a fullness that startled him. He could see the prison, the room, the table where they'd sat across from one another, heard the phrase whispered through clenched teeth: "You're the cocksucker's been fuckin' my wife." It was a long time before he slept.

It was clear to him the very next morning that his days on the Henderson farm were coming to an end. The inevitable conversation with Jake took place close to noon at the barn where Clayton was belatedly doing the morning milking. The farmer looked even worse than Clayton felt, face drawn and eyes bloodshot, as if he'd been up all night talking, which, of course, he had. Lynette and Marjorie were sharing a room now, he told Clayton, but that couldn't last long; his daughter would need a room to herself.

"Don't worry about it, Jake," said Clayton. "I already had that figured out. Closer to Rolling Hills suits me anyway, as I'm planning to do more work on the paper now. But. How you planning to get by without someone to help with the chores?"

"Got an idea about that," Jake answered quickly. "I know you don't have any way of getting around now, 'cept walking. So I thought, if you would agree to keep doin' these chores for a short while, I'll loan you the pickup to take into town, and you can go back and forth in it. Meantime, I'll advertise in your newspaper for somebody to do your stuff."

In your newspaper. Well! That sounded good.

The very next day Clayton moved out, finding a room in town above *MorningNoon&Night*. For a short spell, he drove to the farm each morning and evening in Jake's pickup. Within a fortnight, a neighboring farmer's sixteen-year old boy answered Jake's ad in *The Reporter*. Three days later, Clayton and Jake stood in the driveway outside the Henderson farm house, backsides resting against the broad front fender of Jake's brand new Ford pickup. The older one, just sold to Clayton, was parked nearby.

After Clayton had assured Jake that everything he owned had been hauled into town, Jake said, "Well, looks like this is goodbye then." He squeezed Clayton's shoulder and reached out to shake hands. "Been a privilege to get to know you, young man. You made this past winter a lot more bearable, believe me, more ways than one. Even though things with Marjorie and me didn't work out like I hoped for, I'm still thankful you came to her rescue when you did. Very thankful. You're a fine man."

A little embarrassed, Clayton managed a weak smile. "I appreciate that, Jake. Please know I share the sentiment. But listen. You mind if I ask you a personal question?"

"Go ahead! If I don't like it, I won't answer it!"

"Oh. Well. I don't mean to pry, so if it's none of my business..."

"Shoot!"

Clayton paused a moment, uncertain whether to ask or not. "Well," he finally ventured, "when Marjorie told you she didn't want to share your bedroom anymore..."—Clayton had a sudden moment of panic—did he actually know who had made that first move or was he only presuming because Marjorie had told him she had?—but he recovered and continued, "well, you seemed okay with that. You'd been married only a year, right? How could you take that news so easily?" He thought briefly of how his father might have reacted. And, if he'd been in Jake's place, how about himself? "I'm asking because—well—I'm impressed at how you did that!"

Jake turned his head sideways a moment, staring in the direction of the chimney on his roof.

"Don't get me wrong, Clayton. It hurt."

Clayton experienced a moment of relief. He must have got it right, then.

"When she made her decision known," said Jake, "my first thought was she'd taken a shine to you and that was what had swayed her mind. But she swore that wasn't the case and finally I believed her. After all, she'd run away once, right? Before you showed up. I kept pondering that in my mind. She'd run away. As for my private suspicions, I'd developed my own sense of who you are as a human being, and I believed you too much of a man to do me rotten."

Clayton felt a tightening in his chest. He swallowed, not knowing whether to be pleased or wary.

"Plus," Jake smiled wryly, "she swore up and down on a stack of Bibles that you'd done nothin' but 'listen to her squawk' was how she put it."

Clayton chuckled softly in recognition of Marjorie's manner.

"Beyond that, guess I'd have to say—not that I'm a religious man, not much of anything at all, to tell the truth—but I've always been drawn to that one they call the Serenity Prayer?"

"Ah! 'God grant me the serenity to…uh….'" Clayton faltered.

"That's the one. 'The serenity to accept those things I cannot change, the courage to change those things I can, and the wisdom to know the difference.'"

Jake's memory for the prayer surprised Clayton, but he said nothing.

"My wife's favorite, too. My first wife, I mean. I was married to Sue Ann for thirty years, Clayton, and in truth, we talked a lot, Sue Ann and me. And though we'd sometimes disagree, we never had an argument that lasted more'n a coupla days. Not once. Agree to disagree. That's the ticket."

Jake took a breath, drew something in the dirt with the toe of his boot before continuing.

"Whereas, Marjorie and me, we didn't fight, but we didn't really say much of anything to each other. I think—somehow—I kept waitin' for things to turn out like they did with Sue Ann and me. But finally, I realized that was never gonna happen. Put way too much of a burden on us." He sighed. "Now? I'm thinkin' Marjorie and me were prob'ly a big mistake in the first place. Hey, it seemed like a good idea at the time. Now it seems like an even better idea to call it quits. So, soon as she finds a way of supporting herself in town, or wherever she chooses to go, she'll be movin' out. And I'm okay with that."

After a small moment, he looked up, repeated, "I'm okay with that."

Clayton grunted and nodded.

Jake grinned. "And that's the longest speech I've ever made or am likely to make again."

They smiled, slapped each other on the back, and said goodbye. They'd see each other in town from time to time, Clayton knew, but he also knew it would never be the same.

When he glanced in the rear view mirror as he drove away, he saw the farmer was leaning his weight against his new pickup, head bowed.

Chapter 16

MONTANA 1970-71

Clayton, Frank

Clayton's work on the newspaper rapidly evolved into a full-time job. He'd already become friendly with many of the townspeople. He knew the librarian, of course, Mrs. MacIver, he knew the barber, Lester Dunbar, and his apprentice, Walter Wolf, but now he began to learn how to work a beat.

There was the agricultural supply house, the feed store, and the small radio station, started a handful of years ago by youngsters as a protest against the war, still going strong. At Frank Bascombe's direction, Clayton checked in regularly with the police chief and the mayor (who was in fact the owner of the agricultural supply house), got to know some of the town council and the chief judge, interviewed the principal of the high school, Mr. Hofstadter, with respect to summer programs, and which students were off to college in the fall.

At the principal's insistence, he also interviewed the coach and met several teachers, each of whom, when he entered their classrooms, looked frazzled and one of whom perfectly distraught, apologizing that their rooms were in disarray because school was shutting down in a matter of days: dioramas were being disassembled and turned back into fatally damaged cardboard boxes, corkboards were being stripped of drawings and collages and posters, thumbtacks lay scattered about to impale the unwary: "Careful! Don't sit there!"

He learned the difference between a news story and a human interest story. Frank helped him with structure at first, but he quickly got the hang of it. He began to think that being a relative newcomer—familiar with some things but ignorant enough to remain curious and eager about everyone and everything—gave him an advantage in writing a story. Ask enough questions, and you'll get it right; keep it fresh.

He attended the high school graduation, partly to write up the story—an assignment from Bascombe—but also to applaud when his fellow employee, the fresh-faced, excited-looking Abby, whose black hair under her mortarboard had been permed and whose parents' faces beamed like headlamps in a coal mine, received her diploma. Not long after, he attended Abby's wedding, as well, kissing both dimpled cheeks, pumping the hands of the skinny young man who was whisking her away to Florida. The next day, of course, it was Clayton who would be manning the phones. "Just temporary," Bascombe assured him. "Until we can find a replacement." And it was.

In the middle of June, Marjorie called Clayton at the newspaper office to tell him she was leaving the Henderson farm. With some trepidation, he agreed to help with her move, and in the late afternoon drove his pickup over to collect her belongings. It was good to see Jake again as well. The daughter, Lynette, whom Clayton had scarcely seen since that middle-of-the-night clutch on the porch, was nice-looking, he thought, except for a receding chin. She had brown hair and freckles but the effects of her own severed marriage were still visible on her face and in the desultory way she moved. On the way into town, where Marjorie had already secured a small bungalow as far away from the business district as she could manage, she told him that over the month or so since she and Lynette had been brought together, they had forged a real bond.

After they had crossed over the bridge on the way into town, Clayton looked at her and raised his eyebrows.

"I know! I know! Shocked the heck out of me, too. We commiserated with each other over the differences between, y'know, our expectations going in and how that all turned to mud. Considering that the man I was busting up with was her dad, I expected her to be a little hostile—maybe a whole lot hostile—but she wasn't. Fellow travelers, I guess. I expect we'll see each other from time to time."

Clayton chuckled. "That sounds grand, Marjorie."

It took them less than half an hour to unload her stuff. Whereupon Marjorie suggested they go for a drink at the Iron Penny, a roadhouse east of town, a mile or so past her bungalow.

"I'm buying," she declared. "I owe it to you for helping me out here. Don't worry about it, I got a nice settlement from Jake."

"You don't owe me a thing," said Clayton, "but I accept."

A few minutes later they were sitting at a booth. The place had not yet begun to get crowded. After they'd been served beers and clinked glasses, Marjorie said, "Y'know, Clayton, you've been a really good friend to me. I appreciate everything you've done. Seriously. But I wanted to tell you—surprise! surprise!—I've been reading your poems lately. In the newspaper? They're really nice. Pretty deep, though. Sometimes I have to stop and think to figure them out. But I like them. And often figuring them out is—well—fun."

"Gee, thanks, Marjorie! Nice of you to say. Means a lot to me that you like them."

"Well, I mean it. Never got into poetry much when I was in school, y'know, but I'm changing my mind. All because of you, mister! Your poems make me feel stuff. Make me think."

"How about that? A double-whammy! Can't ask for more!" What was coming? he wondered.

"Clayton, you didn't talk much back at the farm in the early days, though you were always a good listener. But your poems sure speak volumes, as they say." She looked away a moment, then took another swallow of beer and said: "I feel like we've established a connection. Don't you feel that?"

Clayton took a sip of his beer and shifted slightly in the booth.

"I felt it right away, back at the farm. Had nothing to do with your saving my bacon on the hillside and keeping me company while I recuperated. I mean, I know I shouldn't have come on to you the way I did that one time—I'm sorry as hell about that—but still. I don't think I've ever talked about so much personal stuff with anybody since—well, since my husband." She stopped and snorted. "The other one, I mean."

Clayton acknowledged this with a smile and a little dip of his head, uncertain about what might come next, but a bit worried. He did remember the *one time* she referred to, remembered her legs moving suggestively under the covers, and that later he'd decided he was not entirely blameless. But he'd been rock solid about not wanting to do anything that might endanger his friendship with Jake and, in the end, good sense and decorum had prevailed.

"So I was *won*dering," she said, rolling her eyes, "whether you might like to hook up sometime? You know, you and me? I'm free now, and I haven't heard you're seeing anybody. Are you—um—interested?"

He sighed, looked away, swished his beer around in the glass.

"Marjorie, Marjorie. Oh, good golly. What can I say?"

He took the last swallow of beer in his glass. "Listen, Marjorie. I like you, I really do. I'm sorry we met the way we did—especially since it made my muscles sore for a good two weeks—but I'm very happy we did. You're a lovely woman. No question." He looked down, smiled, looked up. "So don't think I'm not tempted. After all, I have 'indecent urges' of my own, as I once heard you admit to. I wasn't completely blameless, since I did kind of have the hots for you, myself, and probably sent those signals. But it would've been a mistake, right? A big one, I believe."

He thought he detected a grudging shrug of her shoulders. Her expression said, maybe yes, maybe no.

"Is now any different?" he continued. "Well, here's the thing. I think you may enjoy more drama in your life than I do. For my part, I'd like to believe that you're my friend, and I'm very afraid that taking our friendship to that other level might ruin it altogether. So. Think you can be okay with that?"

She stared at her glass, turned it this way and that, then looked up and grinned. "That mean you're not up for a little hanky-panky?"

He laughed, then frowned. "I've always wondered

about that expression. As to who was the Hanky and who was the Panky?" *Reaching*, he silently admonished himself. He realized how lame that sounded but could think of nothing else.

"Okay, clever guy. But you're not answering my question. Is there someone else?"

"Listen," he said. "We need to find you a lumberjack. Tough but tender. I'm sure there's one out there waiting for you, just around the bend. A biker, I suspect."

She raised her eyebrows and looked off into the distance. "Tough but tender," she said dreamily.

"Yes, I always liked that concept. Think I picked it up in my youth from an ad for durable automobile parts."

"Well, wherever. Still, that may be asking a bit much."

"Nonsense. He's there. I'm sure of it. Meanwhile, how about a cat?"

He'd been thinking a lot lately about a small black cat he'd once owned. Now that he was living alone again, maybe it was time to consider that for himself.

"A cat?"

"Sure. There must be an animal shelter of some kind around where you can pick up a cat for free. In fact, I've heard about something called The Humane Society of Western Montana, founded back in 1963 in Missoula. See how useful it is to work for a newspaper? All sorts of odd facts. So, why not? Cats are good company when you're alone."

"A cat. Well, maybe."

Frank continued to publish Clayton's poems, one each week, in a special column he called, *The Poet's Corner*. Late in the summer, the head of the English Department at Rolling Hills High, a man named Lipton, recently returned from a trip abroad, called Clayton to ask if he would be interested in teaching a poetry course at the local high school in September. He'd already cleared it with the principal, Mr. Hofstadter. Once Clayton had recovered from the shock and understood that the offer was real, he agreed to it and hung up the phone with a feeling of absolute elation. It was only one course; he'd still have time to work at the newspaper.

Then another shock. Just before fall classes resumed at the University of Montana in Missoula, Terence Bone, one of the faculty members there and a friend of Bascombe, drove down to Rolling Hills to look him up, impressed, as he said, with the "lyricism and fresh touch" of Clayton's poetry. As well as the fact that so many of them were about birds, "from whose movements, beauty, sounds, and habits you manage to wring such compelling observations about life." At the end of the dinner they had shared at *MorningNoon&Night*, Clayton watched his car drive away toward the turnoff to Missoula, shaking his head and muttering to himself, "My 'lyricism and fresh touch.' Imagine that!"

Clayton and Frank began to talk about the possibility

of publishing a book, a collection. "Since so many poems feature birds of prey, said the editor, "why don't we call it *In the Shadow of the Condor?*"

Once he was alone, Clayton shook his head in disbelief. This is what it's all been about, he thought. This is where I was headed all along.

Over many months, Clayton became an avid reader of newspapers from Pacific Northwest communities, all available to him in Bascombe's morgue. Usually at night. After all, he'd been to most of those places. Worked in most. While still keeping a low profile, he'd nevertheless had small adventures in most.

So, on such occasions, he'd take the keys from the secretary's desk, unlock the room behind the printing press, select a few recent issues—more from places he'd been than places he'd not—and page through, scanning for anything interesting. Pocatello was represented and Boise, as were Bellingham, Bozeman, Ellensburg, Corvallis, Klamath Falls, Coeur d'Alene, a few others. At one time or another, Clayton had been in all the towns he chose to monitor.

But the one he never failed to check was Southeast City. And there in that community's *Union-Clarion*, as summer drew to a close, he discovered something that made the hairs on the back of his neck crawl. Tucked in among announcements about the Sweet Onion Festival, the awarding of the annual Kiwanis Club scholarships, and the issuing of new park rules by the city council, was a follow-up article on a shooting that had taken place a week earlier.

A woman—name withheld—had admitted to the killing of her estranged husband—a former felon—and was in jail awaiting arraignment. The prosecutor had not yet decided what charges would be filed.

As he read on, Clayton's breath stopped. In its last paragraph, the story mentioned that the weapon used, a Savage Model 24 .22/.410, was unregistered and—so the woman claimed—had been left to her some years earlier by a person she refused to name. The newspaper, in a flamboyant touch, referred to this person as "the mysterious stranger."

The moment he'd finished reading, Clayton rose to his feet involuntarily and breathed a few short, shallow breaths. "Holy shit!" he muttered. And again, "Holy shit!"

Hours later, after unbroken pacing and thinking in his room, Clayton called Frank and asked to meet him at the Iron Penny.

When the editor arrived he found Clayton in a booth, an empty brandy glass in front of him. After the two had ordered fresh drinks, Clayton cleared his throat and told Frank he needed to leave Rolling Hills immediately. When his boss probed him for a reason, he said only that something had come up elsewhere that demanded his immediate attention. He said he was sorry but he had no choice. He had to go.

The editor looked at him across the table, took a swallow of beer, rubbed his chin. Finally, he nodded and said, "You're him, aintcha."

Clayton felt a cold wind pass through him. "What do you mean, Frank? I'm who?"

"The 'mysterious stranger.' You left the morgue files in a bit of disarray this afternoon. Very unlike you. So I scanned the newspaper and my eye settled on that story. That's how come you feel you need to leave. I'm damn sure of it. But what I don't know is why. Tell me, Clayton."

Clayton was silent, so the editor continued. "If you go, you'll be leaving a very good thing here, you know. You've worked your way into this community and become something of a linchpin, so to speak. We'd hate to see you go, Clayton. Hell, *I'd* hate to see you go! So please. Tell me. What it is that's goin' on. I figure you owe me that much."

At the editor's 'you owe me,' Clayton closed his eyes, slumped in his seat, shook his head slowly side to side. Then his head stopped, but his jaw moved back and forth. He opened his eyes, looked around the room to signal the barmaid for another brandy. He clasped his large hands around the side of his head, fingers loosely interlocked over his scalp. He closed his eyes again, tilted his head upward, rocked back and forth a time or two.

Across the table, Frank observed the struggle his newfound friend was going through and wondered: What in thunder could cause such consternation?

Finally Clayton returned his attention to his friend and employer, looked him in the eyes.

"You're right," he said. "I owe you. So here goes."

They'd been talking for hours now. During the last two they'd been drinking coffee, not booze. Big Arnold Hodges, proprietor of the Iron Penny, had long ago kicked everyone out of the bar to begin his cleanup. Half an hour after that he'd approached the two of them, tossed his apron onto a nearby peg, and announced he was "haulin' ass outa here" and they should "be sure to lock the place up when they left." He'd then tossed a set of keys to Frank, causing Clayton briefly to wonder whether everyone in Rolling Hills trusted Frank Bascombe so completely?

Now, after a moment of silence, when Clayton seemed to have brought his tale to a close, the editor said, "That's it, then?"

"I think so, Frank. Everything about my life that seems relevant. Pretty hairy tale, right?"

The editor smiled and looked away a moment. His smile morphed suddenly into a yawn which he tried and failed to suppress. An embarrassed smile, then his face became serious. He glanced down at his coffee cup, then up again.

"Clayton," he said. "Thank you for leveling with me. It's a pretty wild and storied past you've described, for sure, but I know—I can feel—without question—that you're basically a straight shooter and a fine man. Make no mistake: everything you've told me is information that, as your employer and, hopefully, your friend, I sorely needed to have."

He paused a moment. "Let me tell you something, young man. I like you. I respect you. Now more than ever. I think you're a fine poet—that much is clear—but I also think you've got a future with this newspaper and this town if you care to settle down here. I hope to see it happen."

Clayton opened his mouth to speak, but Frank's hand on his arm stopped him. "Listen up a moment more. I know you're hell bent to hustle back to Washington right now and I respect that. But maybe—just maybe—we need to spend a few minutes pondering what's the best way to proceed." He leaned across the table: "*The best way.*"

Then he crossed his legs and leaned back. "So before you rush off half-cocked, let's discuss for a moment what your options might be. And how I might be able to help. Seriously. Ten minutes. That's all I ask."

Chapter 17

SOUTHEAST CITY, WASHINGTON, 1971

Clayton, Johnny Whitewater

Try as he might to ignore it, Clayton's heart was beating fast now as, eyes shut tight, he rode the Dehavilland turboprop from Missoula to Southeast City. A decade or so earlier, he'd stood atop one of the Three Sisters volcanic mountains in the Cascades, looking out and down at the vast wilderness far below, and had not been frightened in the least, only exhilarated. But this was the first time he'd ever flown, and he was acutely conscious that there was no rock beneath his feet. It was difficult, he thought, to surrender his fate to a machine. He'd been on that mountaintop, in fact, because it was a good place to spot condors in their natural habitat. All in all, much as he admired birds, he was far more comfortable watching them fly than trying to do it himself. But this trip, getting there as soon as possible was what mattered.

He opened his eyes, locked tight almost since takeoff, and looked around the plane. A scattering of folk filled the eighteen passenger seats: a beefy businessman, looking as if he'd been hired to stretch the collar of his white shirt; a mother with a fussy three-year old and a sleeping five year old; and a teenager who looked like a perfect choice for the cover of a Boy Scout manual. Clayton had taken a seat in the rear, which he'd been told was the safest place in the event of a crash. He remained skeptical; if you crashed into a mountainside from an altitude of 15,000 feet, did it matter whether you were the first or the last to hit the ground?

Across the narrow aisle, the man traveling with Clayton looked to be snoozing peacefully. An impeccably dressed lawyer about his own age, Johnny Whitewater was a friend of Frank Bascombe. Clayton's editor had given Clayton the money for the journey as either an advance or a loan.

Although Frank had said that evening at the Iron Penny, "if you decide not to come back, or you're made captive by the prison system, I guess it'll have to be considered a gift."

Clayton smiled at the memory of his first meeting with Johnny, who had driven down from Missoula in his Porsche 911 the next morning. The attorney had told him straightaway: *Hi. I'm Johnny Whitewater. Twenty-five percent Cheyenne, twenty-five percent Cree, twenty-five percent Nez*

Perce, and 100 percent Harvard Law. Frank had chuckled, though he'd heard it before, but Clayton had been puzzled. *Wait a minute,* he'd said. *What happened to the other twenty-five percent?* Poker-faced, Johnny had replied: *White man. We don't talk about that.*

The Indian was handsome: trim but with good shoulders, mahogany complexion, a pleasant, narrow face set off with Clifford Clark rimless glasses, squid-ink black hair pulled back and tied in a bun. He looked more like a model for Esquire than the super-attorney he was reputed to be. He'd made his reputation (and his money) as a criminal lawyer but was also very much involved with civil suits brought by Indian tribes in Montana. A member of the vociferous American Indian Movement since its founding in 1968, he was surprisingly relaxed, mostly cheerful, eternally optimistic and, from what Clayton had been able to observe, a very nice guy.

It was more than fear of flying that agitated Clayton as he fretted about the reason for the trip. What would Maddie's reaction be to seeing him again? Thrilled? Angry? If furious, was it an anger that could be overcome? One thing he became more sure of with every passing moment since he'd discovered that article in the newspaper: he wanted desperately to see her, be with her, to be hers forever. In his mind, she'd become everything.

His gaze sought the window for the first time and he was astonished by the sight. Mountains, valleys, rivers.

Like a colored relief map, except real. The Cascades, seen from this height, were no less gorgeous than they had been when he was tramping through them. The Three Sisters were far south of him now, near Bend, Oregon, but this view was almost as spectacular. And so quick a journey! He'd be seeing Maddie in...what? A matter of hours? His and Johnny's appointment at the DA's office was at one PM today and he wasn't sure how long that would take.

Abruptly, the plane began to descend. He felt his ears pop. Not long, now. Not long at all.

"Nervous?"

Clayton looked across the aisle. Johnny was wide awake and grinning at him.

"You mean about the landing, or what comes later?"

"I wouldn't have taken you for a nervous flyer, Clayton."

"Actually, it *is* my first time, so I am. A bit. But I think more concerned about what I'll find on the ground."

Johnny reached across the aisle and squeezed Clayton's shoulder. "Like I told you, don't sweat it. I think your lady friend is in good hands, and your own exposure should be nothing at all, really, here in Washington or later in California. Remember, I'm here to facilitate, not because I think a lawyer is sorely needed. You'll be fine."

"Nice of you to help out this way, Johnny."

"Nonsense. I was happy when Frank called me. I'm always ready to help a friend, and I've known Frank for—good grief!—more than a decade. Besides, Marshall

Clifford —the DA in Southeast City—is a chum from law school. Frankly, I'm looking forward to seeing him again. The prosecution, if any, would be in his hands, and he's a sensible fellow. So don't worry."

Clayton had never been in a DA's office. Or any law office for that matter. An array of neatly spaced diplomas covered the back wall. A tasteful swivel-chair stood behind a broad cherry wood desk whose top was so neat it looked manicured. The room had wall-to-wall carpeting, warm brown leather couches that matched, and scattered leather-backed chairs. Marshall Clifford was a man in his mid-thirties, tall enough to make one imagine he would have been hell on the backboards in a basketball game. He had a wide and amiable smile.

Clayton watched Clifford and Johnny laugh as they greeted each other. He felt a flutter of confidence from this; but still uncertain, like a child masquerading as an adult. After he'd been introduced and had his hands gripped warmly by the Southeast City DA, they all got seated and Clifford began talking.

He talked for ten minutes, and the gist of what he said was almost exactly as Johnny had predicted. Afterward, both lawyers looked at Clayton expectantly.

"You mean, she's not being charged or anything?" Clayton sensed that this had been the upshot, but he was too worried to have taken it in.

Clifford, who had clearly been through this kind of situation before, smiled at his still puzzled expression and said, "Let me sum it up for you, Mr. Poole. Madelyn Badger has been cleared of all charges. She was arrested and detained briefly while I interviewed her, and after my consultation with the arresting officer, Sgt. Biggs. There were no other witnesses to what happened besides Ms. Badger herself, but we believed her story. The victim had been shot twice on entering the apartment after almost tearing off the screen door, following the woman's repeated admonitions not to enter. We held a formal hearing in front of a judge, the Honorable Horace Gilbert, to bring these findings to his attention, and he agreed with our recommendation that no prosecution should be initiated. He further agreed with my office's conclusion that the evidence suggesting it was justifiable homicide had been substantiated. It was written into the record that Ms. Badger, who, a year earlier, according to police records, had been raped by the victim in that same apartment, was in the process of being attacked by him when she shot him. So no charges were ever officially filed. Ms. Badger, as far as we know, is back in her home."

Raped! She'd been raped? That bastard had raped her? The word had thundered through Clayton's mind like an out-of-control wrecking ball, mostly obliterating what came after. He struggled to keep a grip on himself. Then, as if on a tape delay, he heard the phrase "Back in her home." What home? he wondered. Six years had passed. Was she still in her trailer? Or had things changed?

Now Clifford uncoiled his six-six frame from the couch and stood, as did Johnny. Clayton reluctantly followed suit. He still felt like a man puzzling over a problem in advanced mathematics. This was too simple. The legal snarl he'd been expecting had been wiped out, it seemed. But a far more substantial conundrum had emerged. One that filled him at once with dreadful sorrow, and limitless fear. He licked his lips.

"So you have no problem with the gun she used being my gun? Mine? And not registered anywhere?" He wasn't quite sure, but it still seemed important to clear that up.

The DA smiled. "As I think I mentioned, Mr. Poole, the State of Washington has no laws requiring the registration of guns. So, no. There are no charges on that score. The gun, by the way—which was in the police department evidence room for a few days—has been returned to Ms. Badger. You can discuss with her whether or not you want it back."

Clayton heaved a huge sigh, looked at Johnny, looked at Clifford, and smiled for the first time that afternoon. He still felt somewhat in a stupor. "Thank you, Mr. Clifford," he said, extending his hand. "Thank you so much."

"You're quite welcome," Clifford said. "By the way, there is one other thing, which is not a concern of mine *here*, in Southeast City, but will most certainly need to be addressed when you go south to California, which Johnny tells me you plan to do."

"And that is?"

"The matter of your name."

"Ah!" Clayton looked away a moment. He still felt as if there was a huge weight pressing down on him. And rather like he might be sleepwalking. "Oh, yeah," he said. "My malleable name."

"Um-hmm!" said Clifford. "Most decidedly. I've been calling you Clayton Poole. But I understand your real name is…Travis Mackey?"

Clayton looked at him and nodded. "It is," he said. "In fact, when I was living here in Southeast City, I was known as Rusty Thomas. There were even a few more names in other places, I'm afraid."

The DA shrugged. The meeting was over. After a round of parting nods and smiles, Johnny gripped his friend's hand and he and Clayton left.

"Next stop, California, my man," said Johnny outside on the steps. "I've already made an appointment for tomorrow with the Fresno County DA. I'll bet you never dreamed about so much interaction with the Legal Establishment, Mr. Clayton Poole."

"You've got that right," Clayton said. "Feared it, but not experienced it. But. Y'know? I have to make a stop first. A very important one."

"Ah, yes! The real reason for this trip." Johnny smiled.

"We wouldn't even be here if it weren't for her, right? I'll be back at the motel, Clayton. I gave you the address, right?"

"You did."

"Listen," Johnny added. "Should I be calling you Travis now?"

Clayton considered. "Y'know," he said, "it might be something about the air here in Southeast City, but I think I'd like you to call me Rusty. Yeah. Call me Rusty. For now at least."

Johnny shook his head slowly and grinned. "Can't tell the players without a scorecard, folks. Rusty it is. Now. Take as long as you need, Rusty. Except our flight tomorrow is at 11 AM. Okay?"

Chapter 18

SOUTHEAST CITY, WASHINGTON, 1971

Maddie, Rusty

It did not occur to Rusty until he began walking toward Isaacs, the main street in Southeast City, that the address the DA's office had provided him seemed familiar. It was clearly not her old address from the trailer park outside the penitentiary. He retrieved the paper from his pocket, unfolded it, and stopped in his tracks. Two-twenty-five South Park? He'd bunked in so many places since 1965 it was hard to remember specific addresses. But this one! It came to him like the sudden click of a camera. She was living in his old bungalow.

Twenty minutes later, after a walk through a town he only occasionally recognized, although along the way he passed the college campus that looked to him much the same, he slowed and stopped. There it was. Repainted, for sure, but repainted the same chiffon yellow as before. His old rented house. Bright, new lemon-yellow polka dot curtains made the windows appear more spruced-up and cheerful than when he was there. Were there still yellow roses in the back yard? And the bones of a cat?

Out front stood a sixty-five Ford Fairlane. He noticed other things as he drew closer. A broken screen door marred the picture, like a gap-toothed scream. He shuddered, remembering the story of how that had happened. His poor Maddie. *His* Maddie? *His*? Could that be? By any stretch of the imagination could that again be possible? God, he hoped so! In his mind, it seemed, it had always been.

Okay. He swallowed. I am here. What now?

So many years. And he had changed so much. A journalist now. A newspaperman. Had she changed? Of course. But how much? She was bound to be angry. Very, very angry. And had she found someone else to share her life? He could feel himself trembling inside. The biblical phrase popped into his mind: "I am sore afraid." *No way am I ready for this*, he muttered under his breath. *And yet, I am nothing if not ready.*

Suddenly, another thought. Today was Saturday. Would she be more likely to be home? He half hoped she wasn't there. No, that was silly, of course he didn't want her to be gone! Oh, God! Why did I come? Why did I even come? He drew closer to the injured door, which looked as if it had been roughly mended, took a deep breath, and—before any other thoughts could batter and alarm him—knocked.

After a moment, he knocked again. He heard a stirring inside and braced himself. He half expected her to be wielding the gun. A moment later Maddie opened the door and stared at him through the still tattered screen.

"Rusty!"

She stepped back. In fear? Or shock?

"Hello, Maddie."

"Where on earth did you come from?"

"Well, I feel kinda like the earth just opened up and spat me out. But, actually, I came from Montana. Where I live now. I heard about the shooting. Got here quick as I could."

"Well, if it's the drama you wanted, you've missed it. Wait! How did you even find out? Did you say Montana?"

"Yes. Newspaper. Long story. Can we talk?"

For several seconds she stared at him. Just stared. Her eyes on his, unrelenting. Finally, with a deep sigh, she pushed open the damaged screen far enough that he could squeeze through. She stepped back into the apartment, past the sofa, deeper than he would have expected, almost brushing against the big stove he remembered.

Was she afraid? That thought made him wrinkle his brow in shame. He was acutely conscious of the distance between them. Dear God, he felt farther away than Montana right now.

He removed his hat, fiddled with the brim. "I can hardly believe I'm seeing you again. So glad you're ok."

"OKAY? Is that what I am? How the hell do *you* know whether I'm ok?"

Rusty's lips drew inward against his teeth, but he was silent, except for the drumbeat of his heart.

"You *left* me, Rusty! YOU LEFT ME!" Her voice was a metal file. "What on God's earth are you doing here? Now? Now of all moments?"

He began to panic. "Please, Maddie, I am sorry. I am so, so sorry. Can we sit down somewhere, so I can explain? I want to tell you everything, Maddie! Everything!"

He continued desperately. "All the stuff I could never tell you before. All of it. About my leaving. Where I've been and why. Everything! I never forgot you, Maddie. Not for one instant." He paused. "God, I'm just so glad you're ok."

She seemed rooted to her spot on the far side of the room. Alarmed. Vulnerable. Furious. He wanted to cross that distance, gather her into his arms, but feared the consequences of that.

She buried her face in her hands. From somewhere, he could hear the ticking of a clock. Was she crying? He couldn't tell. Finally she drew her hands away and dropped them to her sides. "*Okay*. Again with the 'okay.'" She laughed, a bitter, unhappy laugh. Her eyes were a fiery pit now he feared to fall into. "You bastard! I repeat: how the fuck do you know if I'm okay?"

She was silent a moment. Then, in a different voice: "Of *course* you know what happened. Else you wouldn't be here." Her chest heaved. "So you know I killed him. There was a time I wanted to kill you too." She took a deep breath. "Did you know he raped me? The bastard *raped* me. You left me here for that! YOU LEFT ME HERE!"

He felt faint, told himself to hold on. As quietly as he could, he said, "I get it, Maddie. Really. I understand." A beat. Two beats. "But can we at least talk? Please? *Before* you kill me?"

He thought he saw the brief flicker of a smile, but he couldn't be sure. She turned and walked into the kitchen. Should he close the door, he wondered? He closed the door and followed, leaving his hat on the arm of the couch.

They drew up chairs across from each other at the table. The same table—he suddenly remembered—where he'd written that note to her. And afterwards gathered up Schorl, his kitten—their kitten—just before he left. The table where they'd shared pancakes he'd made for her just after the first moment she'd tried to pry out of him who he really was. Where he'd asked her to trust him. God, how rejected she must have felt.

He resolved to imagine that that moment was now, the moment to answer that long-ago question as if six years had not elapsed in between. He looked toward the window a moment, then back at her, took another breath.

"First of all, as you may have guessed by now, my given name wasn't...*isn't*...Rusty, though I always loved hearing you say it. Might as well start there. My birth name was Travis. Travis Mackey. Second of all, Maddie, when you shot your husband with that gun, it was not the first time it'd been used to kill someone. And that's what I was running from."

So he told her about the man he'd killed. How young he'd been when it happened. Told her about his father, about how he'd fled, and where. Then he told her about seeing her husband in prison. How he naively believed he could reason with him, to convince him to sign the divorce papers. Which he'd finally understood as a disaster.

After a pause, he said, "He not only threatened me then, Maddie. He also threatened you. Back then. On that occasion. Because we were sleeping together. I knew if he got out and came after you I'd have to kill him."

She reached out and silently moved a salt cellar to the edge of the table; moved it back.

"But I . . , I didn't want to kill someone else, Maddie. And I didn't want it to all come out. My whole story. And it would have. So I figured then that—if I left, if I got out of your life—at least he'd have no reason to do you harm. Turns out I was wrong. Terribly wrong. And I'm sorry."

He paused. Looked down at his hands.

"But that's why I left the gun here. For your protection."

He paused again and studied her. What must she think of him? How lame it all sounded, yet it was true.

Her hands lay folded in her lap, and she continued to kept quiet as he slowly unfolded for her all the other parts of his life that now seemed relevant. He hoped it didn't sound too rehearsed, though he'd been over and over it in his mind much of the time on the plane flight from Missoula, and all of the time on his twenty-minute walk to her door.

When he'd finished, he said, "I came as quick as I could after I heard, Maddie. Jesus, I am *so* sorry. I'm just so glad you're o…well, not okay, I guess, but just…glad that you've survived. Maddie, I've made so many mistakes in my life, but I swear I was trying to do the right thing when I left. Believe it or not, I really was. And now?" He looked away a moment. "Now I have to leave tomorrow for California, to answer in court for my long-ago actions."

She was quiet for what seemed to him like a year. Or maybe six? What was she thinking? Perhaps imagining how neatly a meat cleaver would carve him up?

Finally she looked up, ready to speak. He braced for it.

"Would you like some coffee? Or tea?"

Omigod, was she serious? He had trouble reading her now. He smiled timidly. "Tea would be lovely."

She rose and started to turn, then stopped and cocked her head to the side. "Wait," she said softly.

His heart stopped. Wait for what? His mouth was dry. Wait for the world to stop spinning? Wait for her to find the gun, load it, blow his brains out? He almost felt he would let it happen if that was her choice.

"There's something I should show you first." She paused. "Yes, I think I should." She narrowed her eyes as she looked at him. "You probably haven't had enough surprises in your life, boy-o. So here goes; I'm sure this will be one." She walked to the closed door of the bedroom, stood beside it a moment. "Ready?"

Travis's face was a map of perplexity. Was she about to spring a trap? Was there an infantry regiment aligned on the other side of the door, with automatic rifles, ready to blast away? Even more alarming: Was there a child he didn't know of? He shrugged and held his hands palms up.

She swung the door open and out strolled a sleek black cat. When it saw Travis it bounded toward him and sprang up into his lap.

"Schorl? What the hell! *This is Schorl!* How on earth did this happen?"

"You tell me. First time I came over here from my trailer, the next day after you left, I guess, I found him on the outside, crying to get in. Very hungry. Seems you'd abandoned him the way you did me, despite what you said in that note."

"Maddie, I *didn't*! I took him with me! But he jumped out of the cab of the truck sometime after I rolled the window down. On my way out of town, I guess. By the time I realized the cat was gone, I was an hour or so down the highway, and it felt too late to go back and look for him. My God! You mean he survived and found his way back? That's amazing!"

She shrugged, then turned and walked to the sink, filled a kettle with water, put it on a burner turned to high, all in silence. Then she turned around, leaned back against the cabinet, folded her arms, and stared at him. He watched the billowing flames under the kettle. Feeling the gathering tension, he set the cat on the floor and returned her gaze. After a long moment, her lips began to quiver.

"You were supposed to be my protector!" she shouted.

Travis half rose, then sat again as Maddie came rushing toward him, fell on her knees. She began beating him on the thighs with her fists, sobbing. He gathered her to him, trying to shush, to soothe, to console. This is what he had done to her, and it hurt him to the quick.

"I'm so sorry, Maddie. Jesus! Back then, I thought staying here longer was just going to make things worse. Otherwise I would never have left. Believe me. If I could do it all over again…."

He continued to rock her in his arms and stroke her back. "I love you, Maddie. I loved you mightily before I left but even more now. I truly love you. And I've been faithful to you, Maddie. For what it's worth, I haven't slept with anyone since you. I couldn't. It just never would've seemed right. So I didn't. That's the truth."

They held each other until the whistle on the teakettle blew. Then she rose and crossed to the stove, poured water over two tea bags. Silence was again making him nervous. What death blow might she deliver now?

When she turned to look at him, his heart climbed into his throat.

"Milk and sugar?"

He smiled, then managed a nervous laugh. "You don't remember?"

She snorted. "Of course I remember, you fool."

They were barely seated at the table, a steaming cup in front of each of them, when she straightened her shoulders, looked at him straight on and said, "Now what?"

Chapter 19

SOUTHEAST CITY, WASHINGTON, 1971

Maddie, Rusty

It was a long night. He didn't remember how, or when, they'd reached the bed. After they'd made love, they dozed, Travis waking with a start after twenty minutes or so, reaching out for her flesh again, as much in validation as in hunger. She stirred, but did not wake. At that moment, their reunion seemed not quite real to Travis, although their mutual yearning had at one point moved both of them to tears. Now, as he looked at her, this phrase, like a mantra, circled around and around in his mind: found you lost you found you lost you found you lost you found you. And next, have I found you now? Really found you? Are we together now, for good?

The images of their arrival in the bedroom began to surface.

The uncommon hurry. Snatching at each other's clothing like shucking corn. Skirt. Blouse. Shirt. Trousers. Bra. Panties. Briefs. Undershirt. No half measures, needing the skin. She, wet before he touched her. He, hard long before they'd managed to strip him bare. To him, it seemed her nipples reached out for his hands not the other way around. Did their tongues ever stop working? Their scramble toward pleasure seemed a surrender to something ordained, inevitable. Finally, their cries of ecstasy, torment and astonishment at last drained away into the darkness. Humid with tears, they slept.

Having waked, he wondered now: how much pain was bound up with her pleasure? Was there anger there too? The very ferocity of her lovemaking made him suspect this. She'd cried out, but then had *cried*. Tears of joy? Pain? Lament for a lost past? He had no idea.

Staring at her still-elfin face as she slept, the hairline scar on her forehead, her hair strewn over the pillow like seaweed left behind on a coral reef, he was awash in tenderness. How did he manage to stay away so long? And how wrong, he now saw, to have flown in the face of danger!

He'd been convinced when he left that he was doing the right thing for *her*, but now he saw it as an act of cowardice, one he'd only disguised to himself as selflessness. He'd been running since he was fifteen but that "save yourself" instinct had failed him here, utterly. And now? Now, maybe—just maybe—he'd been given a second chance. To be happy for the first time in his life.

She stirred. Her eyes opened, locked onto his.

"Tell me, Rusty. Tell me where you've been since you left."

So he did.

In these early morning hours he told her of his experiences as a logger—in British Columbia, Alaska, near Coeur d'Alene. Earlier, nearby Eureka. How he'd operated heavy equipment on the steep mountainsides, grabbing up logs to be fitted onto trucks for shipment, or dropping them in the river to float down to a site where they were picked up and trucked from there. Sometimes it was the chains that were dangerous, he told her. You had to stay out of the way as they were tightened around bunches of logs.

Other jobs: in Utah he'd harvested sugar beets, in super-hot sun, driving Rovers Boekel harvesters through the fields. Near Yuma he'd hired on to drive grain trucks, and occasionally—if someone was sick or hung over—the combines, following the trail of ripening grain up through lower California and into the San Joaquin Valley, then up further north, picking fruit, into Oregon, Washington. That was earlier, though. He'd been to so many places; sometimes, he told her, they became jumbled in his mind.

He told her about Montana, about Jake Henderson and his chores on the ranch. He told her about Marjorie Henderson as well, about his rescue of her. He told her with a palpable excitement about Frank Bascombe and his work on the newspaper; how he felt he'd *found himself* by discovering something he enjoyed doing that still gave him time to write poetry. In fact, he told her, he'd sought out Rolling Hills hoping to find a job with that paper.

He glanced at his watch and pleaded with her to tell him about her life since he'd left Southeast City. She confessed to him that after her fantasies of pushing him into a pit of live coals had finally abated (she at this point delivered a couple of well-aimed slaps to his shoulder, and he did not flinch), she would sometimes imagine him in one of the jobs that he'd told her about—logging or farm work, mostly—with his shirt off and in a straw hat, a red bandana around his neck. But her favorite image, she revealed, was of him perched high on a lookout in some national forest, a pair of binoculars in his hands, scanning the near and far horizons in an effort to keep the forest free from fire and—in the process—spying all the condors and eagles and falcons and…whatever other birds he could possibly want to see.

"Don't I wish," said Travis. "I would have given a lot to have one of those jobs."

"Why not?" she said. "What stopped you?"

He sighed. "You have to realize: I was living 'off the grid.'

"First off, I kept changing my name a lot to keep my identity secret. 'Cause once you start…well, never mind. It's not easy at first, but there are ways…there are *people* you can find…to help you get drivers' licenses or other false IDs. Okay? You have to know where to look, but you can find them. And it's expensive sometimes.

"Now I realize that maybe, this has, maybe for years, maybe always, been unnecessary—I guess I'll soon know—but, living like I was, I would *never* have tried getting a job with the federal government, Maddie. The forest service? Way too risky. Those guys have too many ways of checking. I would have been 'made' in a heartbeat had I tried that. Or at least, so I thought. I did *dream* of doing that; you guessed me very well. And I love you for guessing that."

He glanced at the watch he'd placed on the night stand. There was still time. A little time. "But let's hear more about you. What have you been doing? How'd you come to live in my old bungalow?"

She thought awhile before answering.

"I must have read your goodbye note a hundred times, Rusty. And each time I read it I got madder. I wanted to hit you with a frying pan, I swear to God. I wanted to stomp you into the dirt."

He was silently glad she didn't say shoot him.

"Well, maybe that's too strong," she said. "But it felt like such a betrayal! I had no idea you were ever coming back; how could I know? How? I could only assume you were gone for good. In fact, you *said* so. You'd likely *never see me again*. That was in your note! And to tell me with a *note*! Not even to my face, but a note! How could I believe you were running away to *protect* me? Whatever you said."

The anger in her voice signaled him to keep quiet.

"Well, I got over my rage. I realized it was wearing me out. And I decided I had to do something about my life. I didn't want to waitress forever. I wanted to get out of living in a trailer like a goddamn prisoner's wife." She smiled. "Which I was, of course."

"So, since I had a key and was over here a lot, I asked your landlady, Mrs. Davidson—you remember her?—if I could have the house now that you were gone? She'd seen me before and seemed to like me, and she said yes."

She'd struggled to pay the rent at first, she told him, but she was determined to get a new job, learn to drive, tidy up her life. Become a real person again. So she found work as a secretary at a public school in town. Found she enjoyed it, particularly the interaction with children of all ages. Eventually she bought a car—she pointed to the Fairlane at the curb—and she told him with some pleasure that she'd driven it up to Yakima any number of times to see her boy.

"Wow, Maddie! You've done so well for yourself! I'm so proud of you." He tried a smile. "Maybe it was a good thing I left after all!"

She gave him a look that could have burned through paper. "You shit. Don't ever think your leaving made it easier for me. It did *not* make it easier, damn you! I shaped up despite your leaving, not because of it."

"Sorry. Really sorry. Stupid of me." He looked down,

shook his head. Then, after a moment: "So how's your boy? How's Sammy?"

She looked away and grinned. "He's amazing!" she said. "Utterly amazing. He's big now, you know? Thirteen, a teenager. Now that I could sort of afford it, I invited him down here to stay with me but he declined! He'd grown used to being with his grandma, and he'd made so many friends in school, he didn't want to leave. Sometimes he comes down for a weekend, and sometimes I drive up there. He's in the eighth grade now! And plays baseball! For the school team! Remember that glove you gave him?"

"Of course."

"He still uses it when he plays."

She grew quiet. Rusty waited. She'd been sitting up in bed but now lay back again. Her face was a kaleidoscope, he thought, conflicting emotions visibly at play. Then she blew her bangs up off her forehead in that gesture he'd seen the first day they'd met in the diner, and her conflicts seemed to resolve into an inviting smile. She threw the covers off her body and smiled at him. Very softly, she said "We don't have a lot of time before you have to be on your way."

Two hours later, his watch alarm clamored and he scrambled into his clothes, walking quickly while savoring his memory of every touch and taste of her. But by the time he'd reached the motel, sleep-deprived or not, he was readying his mind for California.

CHAPTER 20

CALIFORNIA, 1971

TRAVIS, SGT. HOLLAND

"THIS ISN'T WORKING. We've spent all morning at this, with no result."

It was Sergeant Arlo Holland speaking.

Rusty, now known to most as Travis Mackey, was riding in the passenger seat of a Fresno County Sheriff's Office squad car driven by the large, economy-sized officer. It had been almost two weeks since he and Johnny had arrived and taken up residence in Fresno.

Travis was not in custody. This squad-car ride was an idea that Sheriff Florence Marlow had come up with the day before. It'd been sanctioned by her phone call to the district attorney, and Travis' attorney had fully concurred. "It may be a fool's errand, Travis," Johnny told him. "But it shows our willingness to cooperate. Remember. Our court appearance is coming up soon."

Both travelers were hot, thirsty, and in Holland's case, disgruntled. They had left the midtown hotel in Fresno where Travis and Johnny had been holed up for almost a week, driven west along Highway 180, past the turnoff to the old high school in Tule where Travis had once been a student, and deflected onto the once more neglected Panoche Road. After that they'd threaded their way up through the foothills, past the turnoff to the mine where Travis had spent the most traumatic day of his boyhood, and on toward Salinas. Their goal had been to see if they could find evidence of the murder of Travis' father, one of two murders in those hills that he and Johnny had come to Fresno to inform the DA of.

A wild goose chase? Probably, thought Travis. A hundred-to-one shot at least. Maybe a thousand-to-one, given that twenty years had passed. But something about the effort appealed to him. Why not give it a chance?

They'd driven, it seemed, almost halfway to Salinas before returning to the edge of the foothills. Twice during the round trip they'd stopped, once while travelling west (because the sergeant had spied a location he thought looked promising) and once when Travis, searching on his right side on the return trip, spotted a particular gully he wanted to explore. Each man had scrutinized the road on his side of the automobile, surveying its edges, examining the shape of the ravines, noticing the steepness of the inclines, the tucks and folds, regarding the thickness of scrub and tumbleweeds, speculating how easy or how challenging it might have been to obscure a vehicle that had been pushed off the road.

In the locations that had intrigued them enough to stop, they had descended, climbed, slid, sweated and grunted, exploring the areas of bramble and mesquite for hints of an abandoned pickup with a skeleton inside—each time without result. Sgt. Holland had groused as they trudged along. He carried an extra thirty pounds, mostly around his middle. For Travis, it was startling how much had changed, how unfamiliar this route, once so known to him, now appeared. The highway had been widened, all the way into the Valley, the tarmac recently applied. There were even white lines, and they changed everything.

Finally, when there was only one more long curve before the road straightened out and flattened onto the great valley's irrigated plain, Holland had rolled to a stop on the highway's graveled shoulder and switched off the engine.

"I knew it was a dumbass idea from the beginning," he said. "My God, Mr. Mackey! Twenty fucking years!"

"I know." Travis turned his head aside. "Listen, you mind if I drive awhile?"

Holland shook his head. Vigorously. "Strictly against regulations. Nobody but an authorized representative of the Sheriff's Department. Why you itching to get behind the wheel? We'll have better luck because you're driving?"

"Maybe." He spotted a hawk in the sky. He thought of waiting to speak until it zeroed in on its prey, watching it dive, but knew he had to say something more. "It's just—it's hard for me to get a sense of things when I'm not behind the wheel. You know? I want to see if anything comes to me. Is it such an unacceptable fudging of regulations? Maybe we could call the Sheriff on your radio. What do you think?"

Holland looked down at the floorboard and tapped his fingers several times against the steering wheel. No, he did not want to disturb the Sheriff. "All right," he said at last. "But my stomach is growling, so sometime—sooner than Christmas—it'll be time for chow. That roadside diner we passed. Agreed?"

"Fine."

"And drive careful, too. You wreck this damned car, it's my ass."

They switched places. No sooner had Travis started the engine and aimed the car back in the direction of Salinas than he had a memory flash.

"Right out there," he said, rolling down the driver's-side window and pointing, "is where I spotted the condor."

"The what? That big California bird? What does that have to do with finding evidence of your father's murder?"

"Nothing. Just a memory is all. I'm trying to remember things."

Holland sighed and looked away. "This ain't a trip down memory lane, Mr. Mackey."

"Understood. I'm not trying to get your goat, Sergeant. Believe it or not, I'm hoping to increase our chances of success, however unlikely. Please bear with me?"

He'd driven only a few miles when he drew up at a dirt road turn-off to the left, with a white painted sign proclaiming: THE JETHROS.

"I'd like to take a little detour here," he said. "This is the road that used to lead to the house I lived in. The gypsum mine."

"We went over that back at the station, remember? We did recover a body at this site. Where you said you killed that guy? That checked out. It was when the Jethro family bought this property from the mining company and was preparing to build their home on the site. A bulldozer turned up the skeleton. 'Bout ten years back. ID still on him. And some money. Guess you didn't take nothing from him."

Travis shook his head at this, but stayed silent.

Holland continued: "Turned out to be a small-time grifter named Joe Lesseps, alias Leslie Callahan, if I remember right. Now that you've indicated you were the one who shot him, and since everyone seems to believe your story that it was self-defense, it'll soon be removed from our cold case file. And that will be that."

"I do remember, Sergeant. And, you're right, I took nothing. Even though, chances are, some of that money he had on him was stolen from my father. But please bear with me just a moment. I just want to see."

Holland sighed, a long, exasperated sigh, and looked away, but said nothing more. His arm draped out the window, he tap-tap-tapped his fingers against the metal of the car door.

When the Jethros' large white stucco home appeared on the horizon, with a lawn, a young willow tree and several neatly trimmed bushes in the front yard, Travis slowed to a crawl and, about fifty yards farther on, stopped.

"My, my," he said at last. "They tore down everything. Everything I grew up with. But that's all right. I can still see it in my mind's eye. Every last bit."

A minute later, he shook his head and turned the car around, heading back out to the highway. Turning left, he continued on toward Salinas. But a dozen miles or so down the road, he stopped again, this time right in the middle of the highway. Alarmed, the sergeant frowned and looked at him, hard.

"What now, Mackey? You better hope a car don't come zippin' 'round that turn up yonder and slam into you, or we're both goners."

Travis was quiet. He could see a hundred yards in either

direction, knew the danger was a false one. Suddenly he gunned the engine, wheeled to the left across the oncoming lane and, once off the pavement, came to a bouncing stop.

"What the hell, Mackey? What are you playing at?"

"You didn't see it, did you? I wouldn't either, from the passenger seat. There's a dirt road here, almost overgrown with Jonson grass. Sergeant Holland, we're headed for an area I called my 'special place' when I was a youngster. Figured nobody else knew about it. But what if my teenage self was wrong? What if someone else did know?"

There was a road: rutted, twisting, bumpy. A stream could be seen in the distance and when it grew closer, the road followed the progress of the stream, veering off only to avoid trees that seemed to grow like nowhere else at this altitude. In some places it looked like no more than a couple of tire tracks, so overgrown was the center hump. Travis turned the car onto the road. He had to crawl; clearly no one had been over it in years. Probably, Travis guessed, not since the highway was widened and any entrance known to memory almost obliterated.

He smiled, imagining that Holland, bouncing along in the seat beside him, was wondering at the effect this jaunt was having on the squad car's springs.

And suddenly, there it was. The clearing Travis remembered. The stream, the trees, the golden poppies growing in the bright meadow on the other side of the water, the place where, on rare days when he'd played hooky from school, he had parked his father's old Essex and napped. He switched off the engine.

"So where are we now, Mackey? Looks like the middle of nowhere to me."

"Let's see," said Travis, a trace of excitement in his voice, already opening his car door. "I may be wrong, but it's a better hunch than I've had all day. See that copse yonder, on the other side of the stream, beyond all those flowers? Let's go there."

The stream was easy to ford on foot, as it would have been for a small truck. The sergeant followed Travis with a scowl but without protest. And within that circle of trees, beyond the darkening meadow, behind a substantial growth of bushes that served to completely occlude the tracks of the truck that had made them, stood the rusting pickup that had once belonged to the Clayton Company and the Foothills Mine, the one his father had used. A skeleton inside sported a bullet hole in its skull.

Chapter 21

CALIFORNIA, 1971

Travis, Johnny

Travis lay on his bed at the Double Tree Inn in downtown Fresno, notebook open in front of him, pen in hand, not writing. He hadn't managed to compose a poem since he'd left Rolling Hills. It had been a little over two weeks since that initial plane flight, six days since his deposition, and three days since the discovery of his father's remains. Each twenty-four hours had seemed to stretch insufferably, as he waited for the hearing that would decide his fate. Now set for tomorrow.

He sighed softly, trying not to disturb Johnny, who sat at the desk by the window, drapes drawn against the hot Fresno sun, air-conditioning going full blast, scribbling notes on briefs for an impending case back in Missoula, something relating to the Cree-Chippewa Nation and water rights. What incredible good fortune that Johnny Whitewater had managed to accompany him through this whole trip! And how generous of Frank to set that up, in the hope—yes, the hope!—that Travis would soon be back again, working on the newspaper.

The only good side to all this long wait and worry was he'd managed to talk to Maddie every day, in the evening, after she returned home from her secretarial job at the public school where she worked. And two calls to Bascombe himself. All of them long conversations, too, and expensive ones, all on Frank Bascombe's dime. Not to mention the plane fares, motel bills, meals. He was determined to pay the man back, over time, no matter how much the editor might protest. He checked his watch. He would call Maddie at eight. Three more hours.

The phone calls to Maddie, however much they made him long to be in the same room with her, succored him, gave him hope. Not about his legal worries—that was Johnny's job—but about the future. Their future. It was clear Maddie loved him, was as eager to be with him as he with her. Over the course of their talks they'd decided that she would come to live with him in Rolling Hills. He was confident he could find her a job, perhaps at an elementary or high school, in Montana. If not in Rolling Hills, then in a nearby town. She would finish out this school year, of course, just as Sammy would complete his high school year in Yakima before transferring to the school in Rolling

Hills. Travis loved talking to her about all this; it remained an astonishment that, for the first time in his life, he could make long-range plans.

Depending, of course. On what happened tomorrow.

He twisted his neck, one way and then the other, trying to work out a kink. Should he admit to himself he was terrified? He'd faced blizzards while hiking in the Cascades (stupid to get caught in them), had barely avoided a runaway log caroming down a steep mountainside, had even faced off once with a good-sized Black Bear (luckily not a Grizzly), which he'd escaped by climbing a tree and wielding a big branch against the bear's sensitive nostrils when it tried to follow. On none of those occasions had he been as scared as he was now.

He looked over at Johnny, still writing. The attorney had promised repeatedly he'd be fine, but Travis found those assurances hard to absorb.

During the time with Sgt. Holland near the old mine, and when they'd discovered his pa's remains, he'd had repeated flashbacks to that decisive moment in 1952 when he'd emptied both barrels of that Model 24 into the smarmy intruder, Lesseps. Then unloaded a shitload of gypsite over him when, as he was still uncertain about, Lesseps might not even have been dead. Could he have acted differently? Which was more telling about his state of mind at that pivotal moment, the shooting or the cover-up? Or the other thing, which obsessed him even more? About which he'd told no one—not even Johnny.

For whenever that memory ambushed him, it was not Joe Lesseps's face that confronted him (a face to which he'd only recently been able to attach a name), but his pa's. His father's countenance staring at him across those few yards of space. He pictured his old man as he no doubt looked during the countless times he'd beaten Travis, bent over, grasping his own ankles in pain and humiliation while his old man grunted and pounded his son's naked buttocks with the razor strop. When he and Sgt. Holland had discovered his father's remains, Travis's first thought (he kept it to himself) was: "Fuck you, you piece of slime!" No flicker of affection. No tug of loss. No remorse. Vindication? Each time it felt as if he, not Lesseps, had been the executioner of his father.

The thought made him silently thrill with satisfaction. Patricide. How sane was that? He almost chuckled. Twenty years gone by and he was still reliving the fantasy he'd conjured the morning he'd gotten his first glimpse of a condor—an image of that scissor-clawed flying beast from the Pleistocene ripping his old man limb from limb.

Why had he never written a poem about that? Though it lay buried in his imagination, how could he be certain there wasn't an appropriate punishment waiting to be meted out for it? Whom had he really been killing when he'd pulled that trigger on Joe Lesseps?

Suddenly, he stirred and swung his legs down off the bed, rising and stretching.

"Johnny, I think I'm going out for a bit," he said. "Getting stir crazy in here."

Johnny looked up and smiled. "Sounds like a good idea," he said. "Too bad there's no forest out there to amble through. Though the park across the street has a tree or two. Wear your hat; it's hot out there."

"I know. Remember, I used to go to school in this Valley. And before the Foothills Mine, we lived several years in Death Valley, at another mine."

"Umm. Summer in Montana's hot enough for me. Enjoy!"

The heat was indeed excruciating; the moment he stepped away from the covered sidewalk surrounding the motel, it struck him like a blow from a club. He'd forgotten. Nearing 115 degrees, he'd bet. "The San Joaquin Valley sauna," he muttered to himself.

He decided to walk a couple of blocks to a luncheonette they'd discovered. He bought an ice cream cone and doubled back towards the park. It enclosed several blocks and was nicely landscaped. A canopy of trees surrounded a small, artificial lake, where he found a bench where he could sit in shade and watch birds flocking to the water. The landscaper had planted reeds in one corner and among these a scattering of red-winged blackbirds frolicked. He loved red-winged blackbirds. On the bus's route to school in the morning, all those years ago, they had crossed a bridge over the King's River Slough, where small forests of reeds grew. To which red-winged blackbirds flocked in profusion, their bright red patches, edged by more modest yellow stripes, flickering in and around the tules. He polished off his dripping ice cream cone as he watched.

In addition to missing Maddie, he found he missed Montana as well. Odd, in a way, but he felt as if he belonged in Rolling Hills. Had felt that almost the first day there, he realized. He enjoyed the newspaper work; enjoyed collecting information around town, meeting people, writing the stories, talking with Frank about them, talking with Frank about other things. He relished the smell of printer's ink, the hum of the presses spilling out the week's run.

And he missed the surrounding countryside: the river, hills, lakes, forest, the abundance and variety of birds and wildlife—everything, he'd decided, a sensible man could want. Even the smallness of the town seemed to suit him. Its friendliness. Being recognized and respected. Everything else he'd done to keep body and soul together had been just a job. A paycheck. Twenty years of small paychecks and being careful whom you talked to.

Not only that. Being careful as well to remember what your name was, when you were here, when you were there. More than a few times over the years he'd awakened from a troubling dream and wondered: where am I? And *who* am

I in this place? Oh, yes. Rusty. Or Wally. Or Thornton. Or Slim. Or Skate. And—though it had only happened that once—he'd lived always in the fear that someone who knew him by another name in a different place, would show up to rock the boat. Yes, Angie. Angelina Dobbs.

The last few days he'd begun thinking about which name he preferred for himself. Nearly everyone he knew best now understood him as Clayton. Clayton Poole. That was also the name he'd published under. He decided he rather liked that name and, if everything went well tomorrow (he raised his eyes to the treetops at this), he believed he would hold onto it. He no longer felt like that kid, Travis Mackey. He would change it officially after he returned to Montana.

Maddie would get used to it, he imagined. Or if she preferred to call him Rusty instead, that was plenty okay with him. After all, in every relationship, the partners develop nicknames for each other. Right? Wasn't that what he'd observed? Observed, not experienced. Okay. Right. He would officially become Clayton Poole.

He looked down at the grass. Depending, of course, on what happened tomorrow.

Chapter 22
CALIFORNIA, 1971
Travis, Judge Renfro

"Hear ye, hear ye, hear ye! All rise! Fresno County Criminal Court is now in session, the Honorable Harold B. Renfro presiding."

Travis sat in the courtroom, watching as the judge entered, a large, jowly man in a black robe, coal-black John L. Lewis eyebrows on a broad forehead looking like woolly caterpillars inching apart from each other.

Johnny Whitewater was at his side, smiling confidently, but that did not make Travis any less nervous. He had never been in a courtroom before. Never. Its size was imposing, even intimidating, as it was no doubt intended. He remembered a district court judge he'd met in Rolling Hills who, dressed in an off-the-rack grey business suit, had brandished his black robe and told him, "When I'm dressed the way I am today I'm just like any other man, Clayton. No different from you, or anyone else in this town. But when I don this robe, I'm transformed into the most important man anywhere around, whose decisions change people's lives. The Majesty of the Law, Clayton. The Majesty of the Robe."

The wood-paneled walls of the courtroom were beautifully stained, the magistrate's throne raised on a high pedestal. The stout railing that separated the area where Travis and his attorney sat from onlookers' seats was polished to a high gloss. And the tables! The one where he and Johnny sat, and a matching one on the other side of the center aisle, where the District Attorney calmly removed files from his briefcase, were as huge and solid-looking as if carved only yesterday out of a single, mammoth oak. Very different from the modest courtroom (modified from an old school building) he'd been in twice back in Montana, on assignment from *The Rolling Hills Reporter*.

A stenographer sat up front. A small, African-American woman in her forties was in that chair, dressed in a tailored grey suit with a colorful scarf tucked in at the neck. The jury box was empty. The only other people in the court were the bailiff who had announced the judge's arrival and two individuals seated in the audience, Florence Marlow herself, Sheriff of Fresno County, and a man he didn't recognize, parked quietly in the back row in a crumpled suit, a notepad in his hands. Clearly a journalist.

Travis thought he would happily switch places with that man. He longed to be in the back of this courtroom, observing as that man's secrets were exposed, instead of where he now sat, waiting for his own, multiple transgressions to be aired. What would happen in the end? Would life be restored to normal? Well, what was normal? he wondered. The life he'd lived up to now was not normal at all. Far from it. No matter the outcome—things would never return to the way they used to be.

The judge glanced at the folder on his desk, opened it, silently read a sentence or two, then looked up. "Mr. Aaron, you may proceed."

The District Attorney stood. "Thank you, Your Honor. Your honor, we have before us a most unusual case. As you can see from the brief in front of you, this evidentiary hearing is designed to determine whether or not to bring charges against one Travis Mackey, for an infraction of the law committed back in 1952 in the far west reaches of Fresno County, not that far from the Sullivan County Line, in the foothills of the Coast Range. And, *if* charges are to be brought, of what those charges should consist."

The judge was thumbing through the folder as the DA spoke. "We're calling gut-shooting a man '*an infraction*' now, are we? Okay. Hmm. I'm reading that a man was shot and killed at a gypsum mine? Is that correct? And this was…what? *Nineteen* years ago?"

"Yes, Your Honor. Nineteen years and counting. When

the principal in this case"—he indicated Travis—"was a youth of fifteen."

"And how do we know that this…" (he looked at his papers again, then up at Travis) "…this Travis Mackey did it?"

"Perhaps if you'd let me start at the beginning…"

"Okay, good point. Mr. Aaron. Proceed." Judge Renfro pulled off his dark-framed glasses, ran his hands through his generous head of hair, and closed his eyes.

District Attorney Alonso Aaron, a barrel-chested man in his mid-forties, whose suit was cut perfectly to fit his stocky frame, read the brief in a straightforward manner, outlining the facts of the case: that the boy's father was supposed to be a caretaker at the Foothills Mine, a gypsum excavation, and the boy's apparent supposition that in his father's temporary absence that role of caretaker likely extended to him. He mentioned the arrival of the stranger, said stranger's claim that he had killed the boy's father; the stranger's threats to the boy, and the boy's shooting the stranger—three times—before burying him in gypsite. Then, he continued, the boy ran the stranger's pickup into a ravine and, quitting the scene, subsequently floated off the grid for almost twenty years, frequently changing names and locations. Some, but not all of those locations, were mentioned. The DA had at this point taken a deep breath and was preparing to go on, when the judge held up his hand.

"Excuse me, Mr. Aaron. I know I intended to let you proceed without interruption, but my curiosity has gotten the better of me. We know all these facts how?"

"Mostly from Mr. Mackey, your honor. There are no other witnesses. We did recover the body of the 'stranger' some years ago, when a family bought the mine property in order to build a house on the premises, and a bulldozer uncovered bones…"

The judge interrupted. "Yes, which had been buried under a big pile of…" he glanced at the brief—"gypsite, exactly as the boy—or rather, the man, Mr. Mackey—had told you?"

"This is so, your Honor. The finding of the remains, though at the time we had no idea how it related to anything else, is one of the things that lends credibility to Mr. Mackey's testimony in his deposition. It seemed to us that he would be unlikely to invent a story like that, especially such a self-incriminating one, particularly as he came forward on his own initiative. His account, and what was confirmed by our discovery of the location and state of the man's remains, corresponded exactly."

"Hmm." The judge scratched his forehead and thought for a minute.

District Attorney Aaron knew better than to interrupt him.

"Mr. Mackey," the judge said finally. "May I ask you some questions?"

Travis cleared his throat. *Here goes.* "Of course, your Honor."

"First of all, who is this gentleman beside you?"

Johnny spoke up. "John Whitewater, your Honor. I'm Mr. Mackey's counselor. Should he need any."

"Hmm. Do you think he needs any?"

"In my opinion, not, your Honor. To me, what happened in 1952 is a straightforward case of self-defense, and should be ruled now, as it likely would have been in 1952 had it come to light then, as justifiable homicide."

"Yes, well. Maybe. But, Mr. Mackey, getting back to you. Tell me. Why did you run? What were you thinking? Why did you take such elaborate steps to cover it up? And what about this man's claim to have killed your father? I can even see your shooting him as a kind of revenge, since he claimed to have murdered your father. But wouldn't that have also demanded that you call the authorities and try to get the bottom of it? To publicly avenge your father, if nothing else?"

Shit. This is surreal, Travis thought. In his mind he could see the sinister-looking man coming toward him, pocket-protector full of pens looming in front. *Where had he stolen those pens from? Whom had he killed to get those pens?* Travis could feel the .22/.410 down along his side under the windbreaker, itching to get out—

"Mr. Mackey!"

"Oh, sorry, your honor. I was just…" He felt Johnny's gentle hand on his arm, looked away and sighed. "I can't.…"

"Take your time, Mr. Mackey." The judge's voice was less harsh this time, inviting rather than demanding.

He was quiet for another heartbeat. Or was it longer? *This would be a good time to change places with that reporter*, he thought.

"Your Honor, it's kind of hard to explain. Hard for me to understand it myself. I've gone over it so often in my mind. Dreamed it even. Sometimes, in fact, it seems more like a dream to me than something that actually happened. But it did. I know it did. Only—"

He paused again. "I'm not the same person I was then, of course. I think you have to start with the fact that my father beat me regularly. Very regularly and very severely. Savagely, though I don't know why. I think he thought I had something to do with the death of my mother, though I didn't. I wasn't even along on the car ride that killed her.

"Anyway, I'd often thought of leaving, of running away, just to get shed of him. My father. And maybe—I suppose—I panicked as well. Certainly I was afraid. Afraid of that man. Afraid of being found out. Afraid that maybe I'd done something terribly wrong. I knew what I'd done was irreversible. Maybe I even felt…responsible for that man killing my father. Crazy, I know, but I was pretty sure there were times I'd wanted to." He hung his head, briefly, then spoke again.

"So I tried to cover things up as best I could and just leave. Leave that all behind. I think I just…I wanted freedom."

"Hah! Freedom. You wanted freedom."

"Yes sir. That's how it seemed to me at the time. And maybe safety, I don't know."

Travis wanted to tell him about the condor. About what the bird had represented to him then. But when he'd discussed it with Johnny this morning, the counselor had advised him against it.

"Well. Freedom! Oh, yeah! Wouldn't we all like to see some more of that!" The judge chuckled and sighed.

"Yes sir. I was young and naïve. I know that now. And scared."

The judge was quiet a moment. He put his glasses on, took them off again. Rubbed his forehead. "So, Mr. Mackey. What do you do now? Who are you?"

"I'm a poet, sir. And trying to become a good journalist. I work for a newspaper in Rolling Hills, Montana."

"The devil you say! Good fishing country! Well, you've certainly chosen a good profession. Is there a Mrs. Mackey?"

"Not yet, sir. But I'm working on it."

"Good. Good. Okay, Mr. Aaron. Before we wrap this up, I've just two more questions. Number one is about the father who was supposedly killed by the stranger—do we know that stranger's name by the way?"

"Yes," DA Aaron replied. "We do. Sheriff Marlow?"

The Sheriff stood and consulted her papers. "The man was a petty grifter name of Joseph Lesseps, your honor, alias Leslie Callahan. Scum, as far as I'm concerned."

"Thank you, Florence. We know your opinion of grifters." He smiled.

"So the first question is," continued the judge, "do we have any evidence of the father's so-called death? Maybe he ran away, too—wanting some Freedom!—and just hasn't shown up yet! Maybe we need to wait another nineteen years!"

"No, no! We do have that evidence, your honor," said the Sheriff. "Just recently. One of my officers, plus Mr. Mackey here, discovered the skeleton just a few days ago. Mr. Mackey was very helpful in this, very cooperative. Unfortunately, the location is in Sullivan County, but I've notified the authorities there and told them about the facts of the case as we now understand them. I've asked my colleagues at the Sullivan County Police Department to share the information with us when they've processed things."

"Good. Thank you, Sheriff. Go ahead, Florence, sit down and take the weight off your bum knee. Now. My second question is, Mr. Aaron, what about Mr. Mackey's draft status? Is he liable to prosecution for having skipped on that, along with several thousand of his fellows?"

"Your honor, we anticipated that question. But, before we get to that, I just wanted to add one other thing. We did entertain the brief suspicion that Mr. Mackey might have killed his father." He glanced at Travis' table briefly, then continued. "Not only did we have no direct evidence for that, but the way that the case came to our attention suggested otherwise. Still, I was happy to receive the information just this morning, in a phone call from Sullivan County, that the bullet that killed the senior Mr. Mackey was from a .38 caliber revolver, such as we recovered from Mr. Lesseps's body. And the weapon that killed Mr. Lesseps was, just as Mr. Mackey had told us, a Model 24 over/under .22/.410, a combination shotgun and rifle, just as he'd offered in his deposition."

The judge nodded his head slowly and pulled at his earlobe.

DA Aaron continued. "As far as the draft issue is concerned, I contacted our draft board, #68, and they looked into it. They refreshed my memory that there have been two lotteries to date. Which used specific birthdays as a way of arriving at numbers for those who would be called. The first lottery, in 1969, was for those born between 1944 and 1950. Mr. Mackey, who was born in 1937, was already ineligible, and would obviously remain so for later draft lotteries, such as the one last year. And now that—given recent troop withdrawals—the war is supposedly winding down…"

"Oh, yes! Isn't it always?"

"To be sure, your Honor. Well, now there's talk of shucking the draft altogether. But—in any case—the Board tells me that no attempt to contact Mr. Mackey was ever made. He never appeared on their list. A fluke, maybe, but there you are."

"Never registered, never reported as a draft dodger. And apparently not eligible anyway. I see. Well, let's sum up, Mr. Aaron. He glanced at his watch. "What are your recommendations?"

"There is one further matter, your honor, which is that over the past two decades, in service to his idea that his identity required protecting, Mr. Mackey changed his name multiple times and had false drivers' licenses made in different states to attest to those assumed identities. It's my understanding that only one of those occurred in California, and that was almost 20 years ago, but several in other states. Those are infractions of the law of course, but, in view of the minor nature of these offenses, in comparison to the more important issues raised by this case, as well as the multiple jurisdictions which would need to be involved in satisfying them, it is my view that we should just forget them. Just treat them like…oh, I don't know…ashes to be cast into the river and washed away by the tides."

The judge stared at Mr. Aaron for a long while and then snorted. "I won't even comment on that, Mr. Aaron, except to say I doubt you learned that phraseology in law school. Are you writing a novel? A book of poetry, perhaps?" He held up both hands immediately. "Never mind. Now, on the more substantial aspect of this case, once more, what are your recommendations?"

"My office is willing to rule that the killing of Mr. Lesseps was 'justifiable homicide,' your Honor, so I'm not recommending prosecution of Mr. Mackey for anything at all."

The judge looked away. His face was expressionless, though the dark eyebrows twitched, as if trying, once again, to escape from each other. Although only a couple of minutes passed, to Travis it seemed an eternity. "Well, since there doesn't seem to be a law against incredibly bad judgment, I guess we're done here. Mr. Mackey, I concur with the recommendations of the Fresno County District Attorney's office. You are free to go."

It was, of course, good news. Wonderful news. Yet Travis felt stuck to his chair. After nearly twenty years on the run, this! Anticlimactic. And didn't he deserve to be punished? He had killed a man, after all. Slaughtered him, Blasted open his belly. Put a bullet through his heart. He'd evaded any repercussions for all those years.

All those years of looking over his shoulder, ear cocked for an alarm bell. And now it was over?

Had it not been for Johnny Whitewater's gentle jostling of his elbow, Travis might never have risen from his chair.

Epilogue
Somewhere Outside Bend, Oregon, 2018
Clayton

Gymnogyps Californianus

Above the ice cream mountains
Above the crystalline peaks
dark ravines
bare red rock
blood-etched canyons
chaparral desert
Alert to the slightest twitch
signaling life
and hence
the opportunity
for death

>   or
>   the scent of death
>   and
>   the chance
> for a bone-cleaning meal
>
>   The great bird soars,
>   Flapping rarely
>   because
>   essentially
>   unflappable:
>   Prehistoric
>   Preternatural
>   Mythical
>   Real.
>
>   Clayton Poole, 1977

    Clayton Poole lives alone in a small bungalow not far from Bend, Oregon. Most mornings he rises early to walk to the grocery store, a mile away. His walk is sprightly enough, though he sometimes uses a cane that he carved himself from an oak branch. He wears a hat only when it rains, because he loves the feel of the wind in his mane of white hair. When he returns from the store, it is with the day's newspaper and the makings of breakfast. Including a generous carafe of strong coffee. As soon as he has eaten, cleared away the dishes and his cup, and read the paper, he enters his den, which looks out on several aspens and an oak, and begins to write.

He writes with discipline, rarely rising before two or three hours have elapsed, his only inattention to the paper in front of him if a blue jay or a wren alights on the feeder outside his window, or, occasionally, at the insistence of his bladder. Unless he's working on something longer, he often produces two or three lyric poems during a morning, whether drafts or finished works. Then he is free for the afternoon to read, or to walk the woodlands behind his cottage, listening to the birds. Evenings, he may or may not spend a couple of hours revising that morning's poems, or earlier ones from earlier days. Mostly, he reads. In the last ten years he has published three books of poetry, to add to the seven he had been credited with thus far.

Clayton sometimes imagines that he never went back to Southeast City forty-odd years ago, never sought to offer his help to Maddie, nor tried to see her again. Why his subconscious periodically pushes him to construct this particular fantasy has never been clear to him, and he chooses not to dwell on attempts to explain it.

What happened instead was that he and Maddie, once her—perhaps justified—anger at what she saw as his desertion had been overcome, once his fate had been decided in that California courtroom, were eager to marry and live together for the rest of their lives. Clayton returned to Rolling Hills following his exoneration, and the happily smitten couple racked up enormous phone bills calling each other almost every day, as they meticulously planned the nuts and bolts of when and how they would finally come to live together. The school in Rolling Hills, where Clayton now had such valuable contacts, agreed to take her on as a secretary. So they made plans that she would pack all her belongings into her aging Ford Fairlane and drive to Montana, where they would be married. Both she and Clayton hoped—even tried to insist—that Sammy would accompany her on the trip, but now that the boy was doing well in school and had friends, he'd elected to stay with Maddie's mother in Yakima. They had agreed to send the grandmother a monthly stipend which would help her take care of him, and Sammy would spend summers with them in Rolling Hills.

And that is more or less what happened. After her day-long journey by car, black cat in tow, to Rolling Hills, they were married there a week later in a small ceremony, with Frank Bascombe and Johnny Whitewater and Jake Henderson and Marjorie (no longer Henderson) among the small gathering. And for almost six years the new family immersed themselves in the life of Rolling Hills. The former Travis Mackey had officially changed his name to Clayton Poole a few weeks after the wedding, since the Rolling Hills community knew him thus, and all his published poetry bore that name, as well.

Maddie continued to call him Rusty, however. Clayton was comfortable with that, and to Schorl it seemed a matter of utmost indifference.

The job Clayton had managed to find for Maddie worked out well, and in the last two years before her illness she also filled in part-time at *The Rolling Hills Reporter*: opening and sorting mail, answering the phone, making appointments, and, most of all, maintaining the newspaper's morgue, that same collection of regional periodicals that had played such a decisive role in reuniting her with Clayton.

Sammy, as promised, did spend summers there those first few years, which proved an especially happy time for the new family. Clayton would take Sammy on outings into the countryside, a landscape chock-a-block with tweeting, whistling, shrieking, warbling and chattering birds. And occasionally a hawk or a condor. "If a raptor is flying overhead," he noted to his young acolyte, "a songbird may make short, quiet, high-pitched sounds that won't carry far. But if a raptor is perched, the calls might be deep and loud to rally the troops and mob the intruder." And Sammy would nod his head in appreciation and wonder.

Barely five years into their new life, however, Maddie fell ill. At first they thought it just a cold, and then a very *bad* cold, but when she continued to worsen, they sought out doctors in Missoula, and again, in Helena. And each time confronted the same diagnosis: an inoperable cancer.

Remediation in the form of both chemo and radiation were pursued for a while but proved ineffective. Clayton was eager to try an even more aggressive approach requiring hospitalization in Missoula, but Maddie insisted that—since the end was inevitable—she would rather die at home. She succumbed in the summer of 1977, and was buried in the community she had come to think of as her own. Sammy, now nineteen and at Central Washington University in Ellensburg, accompanied his grandmother to the funeral, and they returned to Washington after spending the night at Clayton's—or what had been his and Maddie's—home.

To say that Clayton broke down when Maddie died is almost an understatement. Broke apart is more like it. The door was barely closed on his two overnight guests, when he collapsed to his knees on the carpet, sometimes crying, often merely huddled there in shock, incredulity and grief.

The home they had shared. The only place, as an adult, he had ever called home. He had spent twenty years on the run, found love, then vanished abruptly because of the peril (as he saw it) to his beloved, and now, after a few short years of bliss, it was over? Was it him? he cried out to himself. Was it something in him? It was five days before he showed up at *The Reporter's* offices. Yet Frank Bascombe remained an unflagging source of support, as he had throughout Maddie's lingering illness.

New realizations began to assail him. How inappropriate the size of their house! How huge it seemed now. And empty. Maddie would never again enter the bedroom, lie next to him. Never again make use of the dishware, the cooking utensils. Never run the vacuum across the carpet through rooms whose colors they had decided on together. In the evenings, if he was not in pursuit of a story, or more often, writing an editorial, he fell prey to bouts of grief and melancholy. It was several months before he could immerse himself fully, with the same single-minded devotion as before, to his duties at *The Reporter*.

Yet whether the sorrow in question is a slow burn or a lightning strike, the bereft ultimately deal with their tragedies, because they have no other choice. Those who remain must live out their lives some way, somehow. And unless those who are left behind are not of sound mind to begin with, they move on. Clayton did finally rejoin the workforce of the newspaper with verve and dedication and, over time, was partly—even largely—responsible for building it into an even more flourishing regional journal celebrated for the depth and intelligence of its coverage. They took on other reporters straight out of journalism school and trained them well. He eventually took over the editorship, with Frank's blessing.

Contributing to his recovery was Schorl, of course, the tiny black kitten Maddie had urged him to adopt years back in Southeast City, now more than twelve years old.

Their cat, after all. Before Maddie's death he would curl up on the rug between them; now Schorl spent the evening in Clayton's lap while he read. *Their* cat.

During the years Clayton continued in Rolling Hills, Sammy—now Sam—was a visitor more than once. He'd become a teacher after graduation, had settled down in Eastern Washington, married, and had two children of his own, both boys. Once, before Clayton left Montana, he'd brought his entire family for a visit. They still occasionally correspond.

Clayton continued to write and publish poetry. True, as some critics pointed out, his work after 1977 took on a more melancholy, even fatalistic, cast. Some liked this new trend, some did not. Whatever the case, Clayton remained within the community of Rolling Hills for another twenty years or so. He continued to count Jake Henderson among his friends until the farmer's death in 1989, and Frank Bascombe was a friend right up until the latter's death in 2001, shortly after the World Trade Center buildings were struck and collapsed in New York City.

Clayton never remarried, nor, to anyone's knowledge—in that small community where secrets rarely stayed unknown for long—did he even so much as enter into a dalliance with another woman. Healthy or no, the idea that he had failed Maddie in some fundamental way continued, periodically, to arise. On such occasions he was pursued by the thought that he was somehow flawed, had been since birth, or at least since his mama had died. A tree that didn't grow straight. A seam of iron ore interrupted by a pocket of schist. A bird with a broken wing, given to erratic flight, when it flew at all.

So about a year after the World Trade Center bombings and Frank's death, Clayton, following an extensive search, purchased the small bungalow with several surrounding acres of forest in Oregon, which he felt suited him, and which he could afford. And there he continues to live. And write.

His view of the California Condor, which for much of his life he had seen as a kind of talisman, almost a spirit guide—and which appeared, often enough, in his poetry—did suffer something of a sea change. It is clear that he continued to respect the bird, but he began to see it less as a harbinger or exemplar of freedom and more a symbol of a dispassionate Fate.

In the last piece he wrote about it, an essay published in *Montana Quarterly* in 2015, he referred to the bird as "an ugly, though magnificent creature" that spends more time in the air than anywhere else, that looks down upon the quarrels and foibles and bad luck of its eventual prey, and whose only task—whose supreme and essential task—"is to clean up after other creatures' violence, carelessness, bad karma or neglect."

If you asked him today about that observation, he might shrug and say he still thinks it's accurate. But that's *the bird's* job, he might add. *My* job is to observe. And to capture—in as compelling a way as I know how—both the grandeur and the sorrow of the experience.

And he would likely insist that it doesn't mean he feels dejected or particularly unhappy. Nor should his choice to be alone be equated with loneliness. On some mornings, triggered by that first cup of coffee no doubt, he remembers a voice—pitched low, but syrupy somehow, and warm—whispering in his ear: "Why not come over to the counter and keep me company? Should it be that the last two people left on earth don't even talk to each other?" And that memory is enough to make him smile.

ACKNOWLEDGMENTS

I've many people to thank. First on my list are Ben Fountain and Jim Shepard, two mentors whose work with me in years past and continued encouragement have helped shape my abilities as a writer. Ben's workshop in Belize some years ago was an important turning point for me, and I profited greatly from Jim's workshop at Sirenland on Italy's Amalfi Coast in 2011. In fact, the whole Sirenland crew has been wonderfully supportive, particularly Hannah Tinti (organizer, along with Dani Shapiro, of that wonderful writer's conference but also founder and editor of *One Story* magazine), and the writer, photographer and filmmaker Michael Maren.

My thanks to the late Grace Paley, whose reaction ("Use my name!") to my first short story over thirty years ago gave me a boost in confidence that still resonates. Two other authors who have since passed on inspired me as I wrote *The Condor's Shadow*: my thanks to Denis Johnson for his novella *Train Dreams*, and Kent Haruf, whose beautifully shaped novels about characters in small towns in the western reaches of our country—most especially *Benediction and Eventide*—I read with delight and wonder.

Huge thanks to the great Spanish poet, Federico García Lorca, two lines from whose poem "*Casida del Llanto*" I quote in Chapter 4 (before rendering them into English in my own translation) and again in Chapter 6. (A single line from T. S. Eliot's poem, "The Wasteland" is quoted in Chapter 11.) Thanks also to the acclaimed contemporary translator of Spanish poetry Sarah Arvio, whose dialogue with me on issues of translation I found quite fruitful, even though, for reasons clarified by our discussion, I chose to stick with my own translation of the two lines in question. (Her book of Lorca translations, which includes her rendering of "*Casida del Llanto*," was published in 2017 by Alfred A. Knopf, under the title, *Poet in Spain*.) On the same subject, my thanks as well to my multi-lingual upstairs neighbor and friend, Jeff Segall, a teacher of Spanish for over thirty years, with whom I consulted on the remaining Spanish words and phrases in my book.

This book was a long time coming, and in fact, it didn't start out to be a novel. About ten years ago I wrote a short story called "Chasing the Condor," which in 2011 was published in poet Phillip Miller's literary magazine, *The Same*. So, in addition to my belated thanks to Phil (who has since passed on) for publishing that story, my thanks to the journal editors who wrote me that two subsequently written stories imagining that same character first ten and then twenty years deeper into his life struck them as less like short stories and *more like pieces of a novel*. So I wrote it.

And my deep thanks to editor Liz van Hoose, whose amazing credits include, among many others, Haruki Murikami and Jim Shepard. After reading the first thirty pages of *Condor*, which I sent at her request, Liz told me she admired the writing, but suggested I rewrite the opening, bringing forward the major character's dramatic precipitating moment. Though I failed to satisfy myself with the revision I attempted along those lines, her suggestion nevertheless spurred me toward a considerable rearrangement of the book's contents, and led to the *Condor's* final form. Therefore I feel a considerable debt to Liz, and I salute her here.

Finally, I'm extremely grateful to the following fellow writers and friends who over the years read parts or the whole of earlier versions of my manuscript or of the several short stories which preceded it, and provided invaluable feedback and encouragement: Bob Bachner, Thais Barry, Portia Bohn, Joel Hochman, Sally Huxley, the late Corinne Mond, Stephanie Laterza, Hilary Orbach, Nicholas Samstag, Joseph Trad, and Evelyn Weisfeld. In addition, Ron Story, my friend of many years though no relation, read an early version of *Condor*, and his encouraging words helped spur me on.

And then, of course, there's Jill. The debt I owe to my partner of the last couple of decades—not only for her encouragement, skillful feedback and support but in many, many other ways—is impossible to overstate. She keeps me whole.

Reading Group Guide

Thank you for selecting *The Condor's Shadow* for your book club or reading group. This section is intended to help enhance your group's discussion of the book after they've completed it.

About this book

Thirty-four year old Clayton Poole has wandered state-to-state, changing identities—Travis, Skate, Robert, Chris and so on—for nearly two decades. Finally about to start life as a small-town Montana journalist, he is suddenly confronted by his darkly checkered past: the love of his life (Maddie), whom he'd felt forced to surrender, and the violent act that first expelled him as a teenager onto the road and changed his life forever.

A work of literary fiction set in California, Montana, and the Pacific Northwest, *The Condor's Shadow* tells Clayton's story in a layered fashion, moving fluidly back and forth through time from the early 1950s to the present, as he struggles to escape, rectify, and finally reconcile the forces that have shadowed his life.

Along the way, Clayton encounters characters who greatly influence his life and the outcome of the book, all with stories of their own. Among them are Maddie, an abused wife struggling to make a living while her husband is in prison; Alejandro, an orphaned undocumented worker who takes Travis under his wing; Jake and Marjorie, a Montana farmer and his wife, decent, caring but mismatched in an unhappy second marriage; Frank, the small-town newspaper owner and editor who gives Clayton a path to starting life anew and then helps him find his way toward sorting out his past; Johnny Whitewater ("twenty-five percent Cheyenne, twenty-five percent Cree, twenty-five percent Nez Perce, and 100 percent Harvard Law"), who guides him over the legal stumbling blocks of doing just that.

Small towns and natural settings come alive in this novel, from the tumbleweed-strewn low hills of the California Coast Range through the Blue Mountains of Eastern Washington and on to the Bitterroots of Idaho and Montana; and from the farming communities of California's Great Valley to those of southeastern Washington and the high country of western Montana.

An emotional journey, as well as a physical one, *The Condor's Shadow* has been called "poignant," "haunting," a "captivating American odyssey" with a "ferocious current [that] keeps pulling you along," and a novel that will have broad appeal, particularly to those who enjoy "a blend of literary introspection and thought-provoking entertainment."

For discussion

1. What did the book's title imply to you before you started reading the book? Did that meaning differ as you read the book and if so, how, and at what point in the story did that begin to happen?

2. In Chapter 3, when he is 15, the principal character (called Travis at that point in the story) first encounters a California Condor. What does the condor mean to him at that time, and how might it reflect his life at this point in the story? How has that meaning changed for Travis (now called Clayton) in the Epilogue, when he is in his 70s, and does that reflect his journey?

3. Would you say that this book was character driven, plot driven, or perhaps both—and why?

4. The novel starts out in Montana in 1972, and then goes back and forth in time as the story of Clayton's dilemma unfolds in what the author describes as a "layered" fashion. How does the shifting of time facilitate the telling of the story? Did it enhance your reading experience?

5. At the end of Chapter 3, after the incident with the stranger, Travis makes two critical decisions: first to run, and then to hide his identity. Did these seem likely choices for a teenager in his situation? In his place, would you have done the same thing?

6. Over the next twenty years or so, the principal character continues to change his name and location many times. In his situation, would you have continued on this path? Could there have been something else driving him?

7. Our protagonist—at that time, called Rusty—meets Maddie in Chapter 1, and the story of their courtship, parting and reunification continues throughout the book. Maddie asks Rusty about his past, first in Chapter 5 and then on several other occasions. Should Rusty have confided in Maddie? If so, how do you think that might have changed the rest of the story, if at all?

8. What did you make of Rusty's decision in Chapter 11 to leave Maddie? And of how he did it? If you were Maddie, would you have forgiven him when they reunite in Chapter 18?

9. Alejandro, Jake, Marjorie, and Frank—in addition to Maddie, of course—are all important characters within the book. In what ways did they help shape Clayton's emotional journey? What did you think of them? Did each of these characters provide a story within the book's principal story?

10. As the book closes, the major character—now officially named Clayton—is still alive, looking back. Most of the book's action, however, takes place in the 1950's,

60's, and 70's. What if any effect did this have on your enjoyment of the book?

11. What did you think of the book's ending? Did you find it satisfying?

12. What did you think of the author's depictions of nature? Of small towns and the people who inhabit them? Did they enhance your understanding of the story, its setting, its time, and its principal character?

13. As Clayton turns to becoming a poet, his poems begin to appear from time to time in the book. How did this affect your reading experience?

14. If you were interviewing the author, what would you ask him?

15. If you were casting a movie based on this book, whom would you pick to play the teenage Travis/Skate/Robert? The Rusty/Clayton character, in his twenties and thirties? Clayton in the present time? Maddie? Alejandro? Frank? Marjorie? Jake? The Old Poet?

Exploring further

In the novel (Chapter 4), Skate and Alejandro wrestle with and manage a translation of two lines of a Federico García Lorca poem. Translation can be a very tricky thing, and the same passage may be interpreted differently by different translators. Well-regarded Spanish translator Sarah Arvio published a book of translations of selected poems by Lorca in 2017, including the poem from which the two lines quoted in *The Condor's Shadow* are taken, and translated them differently from the version in the novel.

If you're interested, you might want to consult her book to compare the two versions. Does the context of the whole poem make an important difference as to how those two lines ought to be translated? On the other hand, does the context of who was doing the translation in the novel (the two youngsters) and how they might have wanted (or *needed*) to understand those two lines also make a difference? See *Poet in Spain / By Federico García Lorca; New Translations by Sarah Arvio*, (Alfred A. Knopf, 2017), if you would like to make comparisos.

In actual fact, of course, those two lines by Lorca were translated by the novel's author, Jim Story, who is also author of the novel *Problems of Translation*, a work that—however humorously intended—nevertheless addresses many of the questions translators face. (See Also by Jim Story, for more about *Problems of Translation*.)

About the Author

Jim Story is a novelist, short-story writer and poet. His well-received novel *Problems of Translation* appeared in 2015.

He has published short stories, creative nonfiction, reviews and poetry in a variety of literary publications, has been nominated for a Pushcart Prize, won a Best New Writers Award from Poets & Writers, and held a residency at the Edward Albee Center in Montauk, Long Island. His writing has appeared in *Confrontation, The Same, Karamu, Folio, Pindeldyboz, Helicon, Aspen Anthology,* and many other publications. His blog, *Today's Story,* can be found at *jimcstory.com*.

He lives in New York City, where he is completing a book of short stories based on his life and that of his parents on a corporation farm in California's San Joaquin valley, as well as a novel-in-stories called *The Hiatus*.

Also by Jim Story

Problems of Translation
or
Charlie's Comic, Terrifying, Romantic, Loopy Round-the-World Journey In Search Of Linguistic Happiness

Charles Abel Baker sets off around the world to see one of his short stories translated into ten different languages and back again into English. Who knew that literary translation could be so perilous? So romantic? So downright funny?

"An insanely amusing adventure that has a deep love of language at its belly-shaking core."

—Gary Shteyngart,
author of *Little Failure*,
A Super Sad True Love Story, and *Our Country Friends*

"…A merry yearlong chase around the globe…There is more, much more, and it moves fast. [Jim] Story is impressively inventive, and… adept at the quick surprise and the odd plot twist."

—*Kirkus Reviews*

"…a zany and surprisingly philosophical adventure… One part midlife crisis, one part old-timey spy film, and one part romance, …a multilayered story that readers… will enjoy." (4/4 Stars)

—*Portland Book Review*

"It kept a smile on my face from beginning to end. Suspend disbelief and enjoy the ride!"

—Eva Lesko Natiello,
New York Times bestselling author of
The Memory Box and *Following You*

"An incredible wild ride around the world. Intense and fun and hilarious, all. A great read."

— Robin McLean,
author of *Reptile House*,
Pity the Beast, and
Get 'em Young, Treat 'em Tough, Tell 'em Nothing

Made in the USA
Monee, IL
31 October 2023